THE DELUSIONIST

By Rachel Mathias

Cover design by Fuzzy Flamingo

This is a work of fiction. Although its form is that of an autobiography, it is not one. Space and time have been rearranged to suit the convenience of the book, and with the exception of public figures, any resemblance to persons living or dead is coincidental. The opinions expressed are those of the characters and should not be confused with the author's.

THE DELUSIONIST

This book is dedicated to the memory of
Claire Eastaugh (1967-2018), who read
the first draft and loved it.

RIP

"I stayed up till 2am reading your wonderful novel. Thank you for writing it and especially for sharing all the truths. Fascinating."

Prologue

June 2017

I can't see the words I'm typing – just my reflection in the laptop screen, eyes squinting in the sun. When I go indoors and look in the mirror, my face will be red and blotchy, with a white shadow below my chin from looking down at the computer. I notice for the first time how my mouth slopes down slightly to the right, as if I've had a stroke on the wrong side. I wonder whether it's been like that all my life or whether it's just happened, because of the shock. We have such a preoccupation with the world around us that it's easy to forget to look at ourselves; then when it's too late, we find cancerous moles, malignant lumps, and it's a race against time. There is a lot to be said for the unexamined life.

You can see why it's called the Hideaway. Women come here for some time alone, to sleep, lie in the garden in a straw hat, pale limbs bravely exposed to the afternoon sun. I wonder what their story is. Mine is pouring onto the page, like evidence, in case I forget what happened and make another mistake. It's therapeutic, Jess would say.

It's the first day of June. I don't remember any other firsts of Junes – you wouldn't unless it was the anniversary of something, or a significant date you were looking forward to. But I will remember this one. If I'm still alive that is. If he hasn't found me by then.

Imagine a quagmire, a swamp of crocodiles, sinking sand, somewhere deep and dangerous. The red flag is up but I stride in anyway, thinking myself Indiana Jones, injecting a vial of excitement into my humdrum life. And here I stand, unafraid because it's not far back to the shore. I know I can make it. Onlookers shake their heads and urge me to escape while there's still time. I throw them a look which says *"I need to find it. It's here somewhere."* A new bride might bravely unscrew the u-bend under the sink to find her wedding ring. A child might run into a road to retrieve a football. But the only reason anyone would wade this deep, risk this much, would be if they were searching for the most valuable thing of all.

The truth.

CHAPTER 1

Good manors

Just a few weeks earlier I was basking in the anticipation of a weekend away. A handful of middle-aged couples were about to be dragged kicking and screaming into what to them was just another fortieth, but to Caroline Holland was the excuse for an extravaganza to rival a Kardashian wedding.

"Don't come before four o'clock. We need to get the place ready," she had cautioned the WhatsApp group a week ahead, but I still found myself passing *Thank you for Driving Carefully* an hour earlier than the official check-in time. However carefully I drove, there was no way to make the last half mile take sixty minutes. Perhaps I could leave my car at the house and go for a wander, sit outside a village pub with a glass of wine and my book.

Before I could even hatch a plan, an inconspicuous signpost directed me off the sun-dappled road into a vast gravel drive lined by tall hedges. I turned in, anticipating disappointment, because these places are never as fabulous as the wide-angle lenses make them seem. The drive gradually turned to reveal a vast Georgian manor, even more majestic than it had looked in the photos. This was more than the website had promised, by a country mile. Two sturdy stone pillars guarded the entrance and wisteria wound its woody way around the front door which stood half open. Either side of the door, sash windows gazed onto a broad expanse of green lawn and rolling countryside beyond. Pulling up at a polite distance from the house (where does one park in a drive the size of a football pitch?) I switched off the engine and climbed out of the car, closing my eyes against the sun's welcome rays. It was utter bliss.

"Hi there!"

The slam of the door had brought a small, trim figure clad in running gear, ponytail swinging in rhythm to her steps as she jogged over, smiling and waving.

"I'm Belinda. Welcome to Highfield Manor. How was the journey?"

We shook hands, hers light and smooth, mine warm and clammy from the drive. I wanted to apologise. "Journey was great thanks. Really quick, no traffic..."

I launched into the benefits of taking the A303 rather than the motorway. It wasn't the quickest route, but Stonehenge has always held a peculiar fascination for me. I am one of those drivers who slows down to marvel at this feat of prehistoric engineering that defies logic and yet makes absolute sense. In another life, I imagine myself celebrating the summer solstice with an earnest band of Druids, while in this one I haven't even managed to make it out of my 1930s semi in New Malden. It was the most I could do to leave my paper-pushing City job to become a teacher, half-way between lawyer and hippie, and I was settled in that life now, as near as I had known to happy.

"Make yourself at home. The kettle's just boiled." Belinda was taking my coat, hanging it on one of a row of hooks under the stairs.

My phone pinged. Caro and James were delayed. A crash on the motorway had closed two lanes and Google Maps was saying it would take an hour to get through the traffic. More pings. Maya and Maddie were just leaving, now planning a new route. Caro was panicking about who'd be there to welcome her guests. I admitted to having arrived early. She didn't know whether to tell me off for disobeying her timetable or thank me for stepping in as hostess.

"The games room is just over here."

I followed Belinda into the vast hallway. The house smelt of holidays, of elsewhere, and tension in my shoulders fell away as the reality dawned that this was not home, where laundry hung neglected on bannisters, where odd socks slipped behind radiators and the remains of Sunday lunch lingered in Tupperware until Wednesday. No struggling to parallel park in a space barely as big as the car itself, and no tripping over teenage trainers while lugging bursting Tesco bags over the threshold. The sight and smells that surrounded me promised a different kind of story. Dripping wax clinging to brass candlesticks and red wine stains told tales of decadence and banquets. This wasn't a place where the inventory was taken on departure day by a lacklustre local agent, and even if it was, then it would be to identify more significant acts of vandalism than the absence of a coaster.

I wandered from room to room, inhaling the scent of wood fires and polish, taking in the scuffed floorboards, patches of threadbare carpet, finger marks on the walls, the unnecessary hugeness of it all. At home, there was barely enough space to squeeze between the sofa and the coffee table, and my bedroom was a shoebox. Here my sleeping quarters – as directed by Caro who was sitting in a traffic jam with nothing else to do … *First floor, second bedroom on the left, lucky you!* were the size of a tennis court, with a roll top bath, an antique mahogany wardrobe, extravagant tassle-shaded bedside lamps and giant sash windows looking over the garden. I stretched out on the four-poster bed, took a photo and sent it to

Harry. He was already online on WhatsApp, waiting for me. He sent me back a smiley face.

Imagine I'm there with you...

My body tingled with unfamiliar anticipation as I drifted into a half sleep. I had met him for barely twenty minutes, and yet he was the master of my dreams, the centre of my world.

It was a whole hour later that I woke up with a start, checked the time and sped downstairs to the kitchen. I was just uncorking a bottle when there was a thud of luggage in the hallway and a loud *"Helloooo"*.

It's a shame you can't convey by written word the intonation of sound as well as the sound itself, but you can imagine what a bright and tuneful greeting you might give a great friend on arriving at a sun-drenched eight-bedroom mansion set in idyllic Dorset. It was a very joyful hello indeed.

"Sal! Perfect timing."

I put down the bottle and threw my arms around Sally, whose delighted face echoed the tune of her arrival.

"Look at this place!" she whispered in awe, as if we were squatters who had struck gold.

"There's more. Come with me."

The house was a delight to explore, and from Sally there were exclamations at the splendour of our surroundings that other visitors wouldn't notice. Along our route through the barn, the stables, the outbuildings, we discovered the tennis court, vegetable garden, orchard and finally the hot tub, which looked strangely at home in a leafy corner of the courtyard. Twenty-first century lives were being lived alongside mementos of bygone generations – a reminder that the human race is nothing but a cluster of microscopic dots on the infinite canvas of time. This was a multiplicity of existences piled one on top of the other. Down the centuries, bricks and mortar had been recycled, redecorated, restored to match ever-evolving desires.

"Look, the original feeding trough. Even the bridles are still hanging up." Sally ran the leather between her fingers. "I want to live here!"

Sally is one of those people who can see straight through the smoke and mirrors to the important stuff. She notices things that give places real history and meaning. Someone else might say – *"ohh look, an Aga!"* but to Sal, Agas are London. This was the country. This was real life. She was more interested in the pantry, the set of bells above the door to summon servants to their masters. I could imagine rolling pastry and taking up her ladyship's tea in the morning. I would have got on with the servants better than the lords and ladies. Too much pretence and insincerity; and then there are the corsets, which squeeze the last drop of identity out of you. Did they do that to themselves just to satisfy men? The thought makes me shudder, but that's ironic, given what happened next.

I retrieved the Prosecco from the hall table and poured two glasses. Beyond the garden, chunky gorse hedges bordered fields of oilseed rape, and in the middle distance, shadowy clusters of ash and oak trees stood alongside lush green squares dotted with lambs. I watched her take it all in. Sal is sometimes mistaken for Charlie Dimmock, and when she enthuses about nature I always wonder if she is practising for when times are hard and she has to make her fortune as a professional lookalike.

"This is totally amazing. Picture postcard gorgeous, even by my country mouse standards."

We slid onto the benches at the picnic table and drank to the wonderfulness of life.

"I know. I can't believe I'm staying here for four whole days. I'm already dreading going home." In my head I was on Rightmove already, drawing the boundaries with my forefinger on the screen, setting the virtual parameters of my new worry-free rural existence, watching the list of possibilities, from picturesque farmhouse cottages to palatial estates, come tumbling into view.

"Oh my God, don't say that. It's hardly started." Sally topped up the glasses which didn't need topping up. "Get that down you."

"Sorry, yes that was a lot more despondent

than it should have been. I take it back. I have this habit of clinging to things dreading they are going to disappear suddenly." It was an old adage in my world of armchair psychotherapy but relevant nonetheless. She gave me a reassuring smile – the kind that draws a line under thoughts that need no more discussion.

"Enjoy it while you have it. So....who else is coming? My sister always leaves me in the dark. Probably only invited me because someone pulled out."

"Stop it! It's the same lot from ten years ago. All couples. All still together. Amazing really, when you think about it." I didn't often think about it, and when I did, it was mostly with incomprehension. How could you possibly maintain someone's interest for twenty whole years? Either they were superb lovers or even better liars.

"Give them time," said Sally.

"I wouldn't wish divorce on anyone, would you?"

"I think it really depends on the situation. Yours was difficult. Adam was ill, it all became too much. What choice did you have?"

"But it shouldn't have been too much for me. He was the one who was ill. I had no excuse."

"You had every reason, never mind excuse. He was a different person suddenly; you weren't getting the love anymore. It was like a part of him had broken away, and you were left with the shell."

"I know, but I still feel guilty about his illness, that it was to do with me, that I was somehow too much."

"Too much? Do you honestly think you could single-handedly cause someone to have a nervous breakdown?"

"Well, yes, maybe." I meant it. A perpetually vulnerable partner has a way of making you feel responsible, the clumsy one who has trodden all over their delicate constitution with spiky heels.

"Well you couldn't. Take it from me. Your marriage breakdown is not your fault. Now cheer me up with some rom com stories. I've been longing to hear what's been going on."

It was always like this with Sally, ever since our simultaneous divorces had thrown us together in panic three years earlier. She had become more of a friend than her married sister, who, much as I loved her, was living in a cosy bubble of love that felt alien to me. Sal and I had a shared trauma, an understanding of how it felt when that bubble burst. Now with our new-found autonomy yielding adventure after adventure, each of us was confident in the other's ability to produce a riveting tale of our exploits, conquests and defeats, which in turn would be met with exactly the right measure of empathy and humour. We were each other's doctor, therapist, personal morale booster, life support system. Eventually she cajoled me into starting the debrief session.

"So, catch me up..."

"On what exactly?" I pretended not to know what she was talking about, but she just grinned her knowing grin, tilted her head sideways and leaned forward, hands clasped.

"Men, of course. I haven't heard about anyone since Jealous Craig and his amazing drinking binges."

"And his amazing empty wallet," I added.

"Money isn't everything."

"You know I don't care about money. But when not having it becomes an excuse for greeting your girlfriend at the door wearing pyjama bottoms and a dirty T-shirt we are entering a whole other stratosphere."

"Not giving a shit. That *is* a deal breaker." She shook her head in mock horror.

"I don't know. Maybe he did give a shit. He said he did, and he was kind of desperate for love, or at least looking after, which I am good at, got the T-shirt. But it was more that he didn't have a clue about what might be nice for me, what I'd think was – I don't know, attractive? I mean it was early days and he was already at the pipe and slippers stage."

"Maybe that was what *he* wanted."

It was true. I hadn't given much thought to what Craig might have wanted from a relationship. But then it was over before it had even begun. Turning up at his flat to find him all dressed down for a night on the sofa watching telly had left me deflated, disappointed, and led to the kind of self-reflection that only results in self-recrimination. It must have been my fault. I wasn't worth the effort. To add to the magnificence of our mismatch, on the rare occasions that we were out together in public, he would drink to the point where he could barely stand, and then would hurl insults at any man who dared speak to me.

"Maybe he wanted me to save him from himself. If he didn't go out, he wouldn't fuck things up. It was the jealous drunk rage in the end that did it," I summarised, remembering hurling the final goodbye over my shoulder. *"Find your own way home Craig, I've had enough."*

"It's a shame he couldn't hold it together, just be normal."

"I'm wondering if anyone is normal."

"So where have you been looking for normal? Or shouldn't I ask?"

Although Sally was just as likely as me to hurtle headlong into unpromising romantic liaisons, she had her limits, and one of them was what she called 'swipey dating'. So I braced myself, took a gulp of prosecco.

"Tinder." There. It was out. I watched her

grimace and shake her head, but grinned back, defiant, fighting the urge to defend myself with the usual platitudes like *"Everybody's on Tinder"* and *"Where else am I supposed to find someone? I only ever meet mums and kids in my job."*

But the expected disapproval didn't materialise. "Nothing like getting straight back on the horse." She said, and my shoulders relaxed in relief. "So what have you found on there so far?"

"Actually, I have met someone who is, well, a possibility."

"A possibility? Have you met in real life?"

"Yes. This morning."

Sally took a sip of her drink and motioned with wide eyes and a nod for me to carry on.

"I stopped on the way down the A3, near where he lives. We went for a coffee."

"And?"

"He was – well, it was like we'd known each other all our lives. I just felt comfortable, like it was meant to be."

This was bordering on the magical, the fatalistic, which was exactly my style, but an instant red flag to anyone else.

"Whoa, steady old girl. Back up a bit." Now I was the horse. I swung my leg over the bench to face the sun, avoid her wry smile. She knew that deep down I was being facetious, and she knew I knew she knew. That was the way it was with people you really know well.

And that was the way it had been with Harry.

CHAPTER 2

A man's job

It was around nine thirty when I pulled into a space on Guildford High Street and flipped open the mirror to put the finishing touches to my makeup before he arrived. I should have been to the hairdressers, got my roots done, at least plucked my eyebrows. I was an absolute mess in comparison to the coiffed and polished Surrey mums tottering down the pavement. I was just about to add another layer of extra heavy-duty mascara, just so I had a fighting chance, when I caught sight of him in the mirror, ambling up the road, nonchalant and empty-handed except for a phone. He had clearly just stepped out of his penthouse flat to pick up a coffee for a tall blonde model called Cassandra, who was dozing between silk sheets in a fragrant negligée, her cascading lustrous hair spread across the pillow. I wanted to be her. Or one of the tottering mums. Or almost anyone except my clumsy awkward self.

He was bigger than I had imagined. More smartly dressed, more smiley faced, more portly, more comforting, less sexy, which is always a relief. According to my mother, attractive men have the biggest capacity for infidelity. "*Never...*" she decreed, all Winston Churchill-like one day after a large G&T and a divorce to match, "*never* go for a good-looking man." Apparently all it takes is one coy smile from the waitress, or your best friend, and they are in love, again.

The parking space, as it turned out, had a twenty-minute limit, so we barely had time to walk around the block. I think that was all he was expecting, but I spotted a cute coffee shop in an alleyway and ushered him in. He protested that he didn't have any money on him, had left his bag at the office because he thought we were just going for a walk. I thought how sweet that he assumed he would be buying the coffee, and brushed aside his objections, reaching into my purse for some coins. The main thing was that we had finally met. We had chatted for nearly five weeks, and not just online, but WhatsApp, long phone calls into the early hours of the morning. He had given me a Facetime tour of his home in Surrey, had even woken me at 2am to tell me he loved me, but I put that down to *men – you know what they're like.*

I still don't know what they're like. I do know that they fall in love easily. A good friend of mine once said "*When men say they're "in love" with you, they mean they are in love with the idea of you"* and she was probably right. But that's the whole thing about being in love, and it's the reason we strive to cultivate that perfect exterior – because in the end it's all about connecting with what is projected rather than the weathered sludge below.

When he said it to me, I should have had the sweetest dreams, but I couldn't sleep all night.

At a table in the window of the café, we sized each other up while talking about I have no idea what, the way you do when you are concentrating on someone to the exclusion of everything else. Even women can't multitask when it comes to love. I couldn't look at him as well as listen to him. I probably talked nonsense while imagining what he'd be like in bed.

Afterwards I dropped him somewhere near the station. He said he had a meeting with a wealth management company – there was an insinuation of tax avoidance. Not evasion, just avoidance, which I took in my stride. He had money, so much money he needed to *manage* it. I could handle that, especially in the light of Tinder Craig who had introduced me to the kind of poverty which precluded even going on an actual date.

I had told Harry about the poverty, and about the jealous drunken rages, and he had assured me there would be "none of that Craig bullshit"; and now he had doubly reassured me on the money side. He kissed me goodbye on the cheek. Later he would say that I was going to kiss him on the lips but he turned away.

"So, do you want to see me again?" He had one hand on the dashboard. With the other, he pushed his Ray Bans up so I could see his eyes. They seemed slightly bloodshot, or perhaps it was just the sudden impact of the sun on his face.

I didn't need to reply, because he had already said "Course you do." Shutting the car door behind him, he stood in the street to stop the traffic so I could swing out onto the main road. People must have thought he was some kind of eccentric who had forgotten to take his medication. I thought he was my knight in shining armour.

I drove all the way to Dorset in a state of high excitement. By the side of the A303 the giant rocks of Stonehenge were bathed in a new light. The sky behind the stones was dark and menacing, giving them a supernatural glow I had never seen. I pulled off the road to take a photo on my phone and spent a minute absorbing the view, while traffic hummed past on the road behind me. Everything was more alive, full of the clichéd promise of new beginnings, a new way of seeing the world.

I climbed back into the car and switched on the stereo. No Radio 4 for me today, it was all feel-good chart-toppers from the eighties, which shouted out that love was, finally, in the air.

Sally listened to the story with the indefinable but unmistakeable expression of someone who is keeping their thoughts at bay, for the moment.

"Well," she began. But then I realised there were even more heaven-sent signs she needed to know before responding.

"*And,* he went to the same school as me."

I left out the fact that he had been expelled at fifteen for dealing drugs and never gone back. I had my own narrative around that, mainly that he lost all connection with education after his parents split up. Left by an abusive violent father in the care of his new stepmother, who was equally at a loss, he muddled his way through his teens in the best way he could. He wasn't likely to be an A grade student with that start in life. Hardly surprising he ended up on the wrong side of the law.

"Incredible, Rach. It must be fate."

She was right to mock me. Next thing I'd be telling her what a great match Libra and Leo were, or what a coincidence it was that we both liked going out in the rain.

"Well, as long as you're careful. I know what you're like. You go rushing into things, but you don't need to invest so much, so soon. I mean I get why you do it. We all do it. It's like a need to erase your mistakes, to find someone new to justify why it never worked out with anyone else. We're all looking for *the one*."

"You saying I'm living in a fairy tale? I mean you're probably right..."

It had been like losing a limb. Not waking up in hospital after a near-fatal accident too relieved to be alive to care about the missing leg, but living with the fact that I had made the deliberate and reasoned decision to have it removed. The amputation of my relationship was carried out deliberately and advisedly, after the pain became so great that the decision was inevitable. It was the recommendation of the professionals, the only conceivable next step. The limb was dead. Once removed, it plagued me with its absence and my soul howled in grief at a bereavement which made no sense. The sense of acute loss was what drove me online, to swiping right and left until I was out of options. I saw possibilities in the impossible, and projected onto my unsuspecting victims the whole drama of my emptiness. *Fill me up. Make me whole again.* I never said anything that gave away my unfinishedness, but they could all, surely, tell.

Sally was deep in thought. It was a moment of mutual reflection. She looked up at me and I couldn't read her expression, but it seemed concerned.

"I suppose I'm just thinking we need to accept the stuff that happened in the past with the other people in our lives, not just bury it by plonking a new person in their place and starting a dreamy romance with them. It's like slapping new wallpaper on top of the old stuff. You gotta spend a bit of time with the scraper, and then fill the holes, sandpaper…"

"Is that a metaphor for therapy?"

"Maybe, or yoga, or just time out, alone. I don't think you can hurry the healing and learning process."

"Sal, what have you been reading?"

"Oh all sorts. Well you know my situation. I take all the help I can get."

"But you don't do the online dating thing?"

"What bothers me is how do you know anything about them when you have no connection to them? Can't you meet people some other way?"

"Do we know anything about *anyone*?" I countered. "And we change. I thought I knew Adam, and either I didn't, or he changed, because he's nothing like the person I thought I was marrying."

"Or you changed? Of course that's bound to happen over time, but it seems worse knowing absolutely nothing. It's like you're deliberately putting yourself at a disadvantage from the outset. I'd just rather it was through an activity where you meet by chance."

"What, like an evening class? I haven't got time to hang around adult education venues learning things I'm not interested in, just to meet a man."

"You could do car maintenance. That might even be useful."

"Well first of all I don't think car maintenance even exists anymore because cars are pretty much run by computers. And even if it does, it's probably full of women with the same idea, all disappointed when the men don't turn up, which they don't, because they already know everything about cars, or even if they don't know everything, then they're not going to admit they need lessons, and especially not lessons with girls." I paused for breath and pushed my glass aside. That was far too long a sentence and I blamed the alcohol.

"Ok, fair enough, Tinder wins."

Sally moved round to maximise the impact of the sun's lingering rays and turned the conversation to the reason for our meeting, which was that her little sister was about to become officially old, just as we all had done when turning thirty, and probably twenty. Having passed the fourth decade landmark some time ago, Sally and I were struggling to understand its significance. My thirties had passed in a flash of relay-parenting and work-life juggling, and the first years of my forties were looking like a kink in the hosepipe of my life. It was the decade of the break-up of my marriage, my husband's mental breakdown and the subsequent loss of my job. It was the decade of selling the family home and downsizing to the neighbouring postcode, giving up foreign holidays, swapping Waitrose for Lidl, River Café for Wetherspoons. So far it had been a catalogue of sickness and decline, sadness, and upheaval, and I couldn't wait for it to be behind me.

We debated the demise of past relationships, the patterns in behaviour which led to unhappy outcomes, "*You invest too much too soon*" and "*You deserve better*" and finally reached the ultimate question, which was whether to take our long-sleeved tops off to reveal the flimsy camisoles and flabby arms underneath. After much agonising, we decided to risk it but only until the rest of the guests arrived.

Then, our conversation finally turned to Sally's latest boyfriend, whose estranged wife and children were completely unaware that he had set up home with another family. I was on safe ground now in terms of tit for tat finger-wagging. And my concern for her followed hot on the heels of hers for me.

"He's got to tell his ex, hasn't he?" I brought my glass down onto the table with a little more force than required. "I mean where does this go otherwise? He can't go away with you, you can't have a holiday, even a whole weekend together, if *she* thinks he's staying with his school friend, having a bit of time and space or whatever he's told her". I had said it all before, and I knew the answer.

“He doesn't want to rock the boat. Upset the kids.”

“So wait until he's free. You're worth making a proper decision for you know Sal. So show him you're worth it.”

Sally thought for a second, then sighed, because all roads led to the same place.

"You don't know him like I do, Rach. We have something amazing between us. I kind of understand why he wouldn't want to take any major steps. It's early days. I'm happy with things the way they are."

This wasn’t the first time that a friend had stepped in to point out the masochism behind her situation, and Sally had her responses ready, which she would fire back in a series of killer return volleys that sent her opponent scuttling around the base line. She was trained for this. I tried what I thought might be a new angle, the judge’s summary at the end of a trial. Girls do this for each other’s good, because when you’re in it, you can’t always see it. We stand on the edge of the swamp because we have a better view of the crocodiles from there. I was happy to point them all out.

“Okay, so basically you are voluntarily putting your whole life on hold, with someone who hasn’t introduced you to any friend or family member in the year you’ve been together, who disappears into the car and drives up the road every night, to "talk to the kids," who won't leave his phone on the table even to go to the bathroom, and all that just so you can have *sex*?"

"Haven't you done that before? Fallen for someone who belongs to someone else?"

There was a pause, the first one in an hour of fervent chatter. It was a fair comment. Out of context, but perhaps the context was irrelevant.

"That was ages ago, and different. He didn't belong to her *anymore...*"

"Maybe. But every relationship is different. Graham and I have a connection. We laugh together. *So* much." I had met him twice, briefly, and struggled to imagine him cracking a smile, let alone a giggle, but gave her the benefit of the doubt.

"So, it's for sex *and* laughter then. Actually, that's not such a bad result... I like the fact you say it's that you laugh together, rather than he makes you laugh. So many women seem to expect some sort of court jester, where the real fun is when you both find each other funny."

My detective alter-ego was still working in the background on solving the mystery of the late-night phone calls. "Maybe you should get a neighbour to listen to his secret conversations. Just happen to be walking the dog past his car where he's having a chat."

"What do you mean?" Her smile disappeared.

"I mean, when he goes off to talk to the kids, she could listen and see if that's what he's really doing."

"Spy on him you mean?"

"Oh Sal, I don't know." I frowned. "I just worry about his 'situation' with the ex, and what exactly she thinks is going on. I mean, when someone says they have left their wife, what proof do we have that that's true?"

"The fact he lives with me? Sleeps with me?"

"In my experience that is no proof at all."

There was a pause. Sally looked into the distance for a minute, chewing over the imaginary scenario I had put before her.

"I see why you're worried Rach. You've been through all this before, you think men can't be trusted. And I think the same about your new guy. Wait till you know him better before you put all your eggs in one basket. Divorce is not a label of shame. Enjoy the freedom."

"I've had enough of the freedom, enough of the poverty stricken, guitar-strumming Lotharios pining after some long-lost ex." I had somehow managed to cram all my romantic adventures into one sentence.

"Fair enough. I haven't had the pleasure. But show me a divorced man with cash and I'll show you an ex-wife who hasn't done her job properly. I honestly believe Graham is a good guy. He used to work on oil rigs, all over the world. He's disciplined, resilient, reliable.

"And used to spending months away from the people he loves. He might have just told her he's working away for a while."

"Well, when you put it like that...."

"Sorry, it's only because I care about you." I tried to wrap her in a hug but she wriggled free.

"Okay, so to take this page-turner to its bunny-boiling conclusion, I need to go and knock on Sylvia's door at the top of the cul-de-sac, ask her to take someone's dog for a walk and hover by his car while he talks to his kids on the phone. Do I ask her to leave a bugging device on a nearby lamp post and Bluetooth it straight down to my place? Or do I sit in the back of a van down the road with a team of hit men ready to leap out and arrest him for telling the wrong bedtime story?"

"Count me in for the van." I said.

"Seriously, you think there is more to this? I don't think he's got the nous to be deceitful. I mean, why bother?" She drained her glass and looked up at me, needing something I couldn't give. My answer was simple.

"I don't care *why*, I just care *if* he is being deceitful. His end-game is of no interest to me. But if he is leading a double life, or hiding anything from you, you might as well know now. And walking a dog can be done any time of the day or night. You would never suspect if you were him, it could just be accidental over-hearing."

"And it may never happen, because I might not ask, and she might not agree, and Graham might choose that day to make the call somewhere else, and the weather might turn cold..."

I nodded. This was all true, and I concluded, as she probably had, that this was nothing but the pie in the sky dream of someone who'd watched too many mini-series thrillers.

Then out of nowhere there was the sudden roar of a car engine, probably not sudden, but when you stop laughing loudly, any other noise sounds like it's just started. We scrambled for our clothes lest anyone should spot our bingo wings and run for the hills. It's madness but we all do it, because it wouldn't do to be judged, unless of course you were judged the winner in which case please go ahead, judge away.

Over the next hour, a procession of cars spilt out freshly manicured couples clutching suitcases, presents, boxes of wine. The air was filled with whoops of delight at the Aga as newly agile weekenders scurried to locate the best room, under the guise of simply marvelling at the delightfulness of everything; London mice escaping their miniature dwellings to discover what kind of square footage they could trade it in for, one day, when the kids left home...

Maya arrived with Maddie in tow. Simon had pulled out, or perhaps had never been in, but this was normal for them. Maddie was a more than adequate replacement, with her unique abundance of energy there was no danger of things getting boring. She was already busy hanging up the birthday bunting and handing out balloons to anyone who would take them.

"Come on everyone. Let's get this place looking fabulous."

Maya was still making excuses for her absent husband. “It’s so rude of him. Although to be honest, soooo much nicer for me not to have him here.” She was untangling a piece of ribbon to string the balloons up with , and just getting it more and more tangled in the process. It was a micro-representation of her and Simon's relationship.

“He never comes to anything anymore,” said Maddie in between puffs. “It’s a shame really. He will really be missing out this weekend.”

“He hates people. Or maybe it’s just me he hates. He probably has a whale of a time when I’ve gone out.”

“I’m not sure about that." I was trying to picture Simon turning the music up, cracking open some beers and dancing round the kitchen. "I can't imagine it."

“Okay maybe not what I’d call a whale of a time. Depends how you’d describe watching back-to-back replays on Dave Ja vu.”

Maddie cackled and then whooped as the front door creaked open once again.

“Jess!” She threw her arms round the next arrival, then her partner Jason, taking their bags off them, then leaping up the stairs in front of them to show them their room. Everyone knows they can always go off duty when Maddie’s around.

“Don’t worry Jason, there’s a gym in the barn so you can work on those big guns of yours…”.

“Do I have to? I thought I was on holiday.”

"Don't let yourself go. You two are like the model couple, all young and loved up. You can't destroy that fantasy."

“What’s she been on?” he asked, over his shoulder.

“Balloons, most recently anyway. Here, help me out blowing these up.” I shouted my last words up the stairs and his voice came back faintly.

"Can I unpack first? Or at least have a drink?"

Presents for the still absent Caro were being placed on the dining table, all shapes and sizes, tied with ribbons and even more balloons and the house was awash with chatter and laughter. At that moment, everything was truly perfect. I went upstairs to find a jumper and looked out at the sunset feeling something approaching true bliss.

"Wow! Can we swap rooms?" I turned around to see Jess in the doorway, looking non-plussed at the sight of my luxurious accommodation.

"You definitely cannot swap" I retorted, hurling myself onto the bed with a *ta dah!* She threw a pillow at me and I threw it back.

"Makes you think, why do we put up with tiny cramped city houses?"

"Because that's where we work and earn money." I recited that line without conviction.

"People work in the countryside too." Jess sat on the edge of the chaise longue and took a sip of her wine.

"Yes, but no-one can afford to live here. That's why they rent it out isn't it?"

"I'm sure there's a way of making money outside the city Rach. If you really want to."

"Wow! I absolutely *love* it here!" Maddie exploded into the room, She had probably never touched drugs, but she went around looking high as a kite, just on life. Jess was gazing out of the window with a serene faraway look in her eyes. She was, like me, a druid in training, but unlike me, looked the part. Cascading dark curls and kaftans were her trademark. While Sally was busy earning money by looking like the host of a nature programme, Jess would be most likely telling fortunes at festivals. She wasn't exuberant like Maddie but just blissed out, as if she was privy to some heavenly secret.

Uncomfortable with serenity, Maddie tossed a pillow in Jess' direction. She returned it with a neat flick of her wrist, and now Maddie was throwing the whole lot back in a feathery bombardment. Jess found her inner warrior and soon Maddie was climbing into bed, burying herself in duvet. Her little face looked out like a happy moon.

"Get Maya and Sally in here, and we'll see how many we can fit in..."

Before we could find out, Caro and James arrived to a fanfare of welcome that made me wonder if there had been no accident at all, just a rethink on the whole triumphant entrance plan. There was no actual reason for them to arrive before us. Dinner, after all, had been pre-arranged. I had taken it upon myself to make a chilli the night before, so that was what we had. A hot chilli on a hot day when really there should have been a barbecue, but the iPhone weather app had predicted cloud and 15 degrees, and a barbecue is a man's job, everyone knows that. As usual, I apologised too much, first for taking the easy option on menu choice, then for the fact that there was too much cumin in the chilli. Maya had watched me make it the night before, telling me to go easy, just a pinch of.... Oh too late..."

I was never good at moderation. You might have worked that out by now.

Wine helps relieve the urge to apologise. More wine makes you even more relaxed. I had intended to stay off the booze that night and be ready for the big banquet the following day, but intentions are only intentions, and are often foolishly conceived without proper consideration of likely temptations and circumstances. So it was hardly surprising that I let the wine flow in my direction until fatigue took over and sent me to my four poster where I propped myself up on my pillows and opened WhatsApp, leaving the birthday girl opening her mountain of gifts to a chorus of oohs and ahs and *"well I just saw it and thought of you..."*.

So what do you think of this? His message read.

I was looking at a photo of a motorbike – a bright green Kawasaki. To be exact, it was a photo of Harry on the bike, in what looked like somebody's garage.

Nice. Today's purchase?

Yep. It should tide me over until the Ducati replacement arrives

Replacement?

The accident, remember? I told you.

Oh yes sorry. Chastised, I wanted to soften the

sharp words with my own gentle ones.

Come down here on it. I want to see you.

He sent a surprised face.

Okay, too soon. Sorry, must be the wine talking. Why was I incapable of letting things happen at their own pace?

It's not too soon, just – well firstly I have to get some adjustments made so it's going into the garage, but don't you need to do your thing with your crew?

My crew? Okay, I spose so.

I'm missing you babe.

I sent him a kissy face back, and then he called, and we chatted for another hour, about me, him, and the magic that bound us. I said I wished he could be here, to see it. I meant to see *me.* We talked again when I woke up. We were linked by an invisible cord, and every so often one of us tugged at it to check the other was holding on. Since we had met, the tug was becoming more frequent; we wanted to see each other again, it was just a question of when. The excitement was stomach-churning. I didn't remember feeling like this ever before.

CHAPTER 3

Danger of death

Next morning, leaving the boys at the gym in the care of resident personal trainer Jason, we walked off our hangovers, 14,834 steps of walking to be precise, which was the length of the journey to and from Lawrence of Arabia's house. T. E. Lawrence had led a colourful life, culminating in ten or so years at Clouds Hill, the tiniest cottage in the world, now the tiniest heritage site in the world. It's amazing how long you can stand in such a minute space, taking in the smallness, the quirkiness of the building and the man that lived there, imagining his mind, his thoughts, his dreams, the shock when he was killed in a motorbike accident on a country lane just two months after leaving the army. A motorbike accident. Everything made me think of Harry.

We were all rather subdued as we began the walk back. Caro, Maddie and Jess decided to take the main road, while the rest of us took a short cut home, which turned out to be a gross misdescription. Maya was a keen walker, a keen everything-er really, just like Maddie but not as mad, as Sally summed her up once, but the walking was becoming an obsession. She walked three miles to work every day and was no stranger to a twenty thousand daily step count. Sally wasn't afraid of a good hike either, but that didn't make us skilled navigators. My suggestion of using the sun was met by shrugs and fingers pointing skywards at the blanket of unyielding cloud, and my "gut feeling" only sent the others striding in the opposite direction.

After an hour we found ourselves at Boddington Camp, Lawrence of Arabia's local military training zone, jumping at the sound of distant gunshots while attempting to consult an offline Google Maps app. Eventually we arrived at a kind of tank exercise park. Huge armoured vehicles roared past us on sandy roads, camouflaged officers waving from the cockpit. The noise was deafening, frightening, heart-stopping in the literal and metaphorical sense. I thought of Mr Lawrence commuting here from his cottage, and then of Josh, my youngest, with his new passion for the cadet force and his dreams of joining the RAF. I have no understanding of the desire to go to war, yet as long as there are people who think otherwise, pacifists are forced to accept it as a reality, and ultimately to be grateful for those who risk their lives for peace. War begets peace. That is so ironic.

And here they were in front of us, going through their manoeuvres with a cheery wave to the onlookers behind the barbed wire fence. Young men in killing machines, life and death played out before us like opposing demons, each waiting for the other to give way. We stood there, mesmerised, awe-struck, and underneath that there was a small voice of protest that couldn't be heard above the rumble of the engines. It reminded me of something I'd read somewhere. *Every man that dies at the hands of enemy fire was once a baby in his mother's arms. We are not born bad.* I'm not so sure now. Some people choose a path in life that defies explanation.

"***Danger of death***". Peeling ourselves away from the display of military zeal, we found that the yellow warning sign at the entrance to the public footpath had fallen flat on its back. This was a social network photo opportunity, and I don't miss those if I can possibly help it. Apart from being great for the stomach muscles, laughter disarms you, leaves you in a state of helplessness. The best thing of all is other people laughing. I think I only ever managed about ten seconds of the Laughing Policeman before it set me off. It's like the opposite of the Railway Children. I am easily triggered.

After a brief photo stop, we took that path, the one that said Danger of Death. But then some would say I always take that path. And I would say in response that it's the danger of death that makes us feel alive.

Maya wanted the low-down on Harry. Sally filled her in, but not in nearly enough detail for my liking. I embellished her account with sprinklings of fairy dust.

"He's just what I need, a *real man*."

"You mean an alpha male?"

"I don't know about that. I mean I feel protected, I'm his girl. He's always taking care of me, thinking about me, making sure I'm okay."

"Sounds like some sort of gangster. What does he do, for a job?"

I gave my speech, probably word for word as he had delivered it to me. I was on message, a campaigner, his girl Friday.

"So...." I hate starting sentences with "so". It's a phenomenon that I swore I'd never join in with but I find myself doing it the whole time. It's the same with "anytime soon". When did that suddenly become a thing? And when did we start talking about things being "a thing?"

"So," (ouch) "he is an app developer. He has an office in Liverpool Street, and a team of people working on a ticketing app for the FA, which allows season ticket holders to sell their tickets on a game by game basis, so that the club is notified of the identity of everyone in the ground at any time. The idea is that the app is eventually rolled out to all clubs across the country. So, there is an anti-terrorism angle, and it has some insurance consequences as well, because the club knows exactly who is in the ground at any one time. Reduces their insurance premiums. Everyone wins."

I drifted off, realising I couldn't remember exactly how the club would know who was there, and what was to prevent people just lending a local terrorist their ticket for the day. It wasn't watertight. I needed to ask Harry more about it before trying to launch the PR campaign. I was trying to justify his existence again, and I had been there before, jumping up and down with excitement about some new man I hardly knew. I knew how it must come across. I should, as my children often told me, *calm down*.

Needless to say, the girls were less concerned about the mechanics of the app function and more about the personal stuff.

"What about kids?" asked Maya.

"Three, I think."

"Same mother?"

"Two different mothers, never married them, but he gets on with them both, which makes a change."

That was true. I had made it a priority not to meet anyone who held grudges against my predecessors. Faced with men who did this, and Jealous Craig had been one of them, my reaction would always be to tell them I was no better than the ex-wife, that I would probably have reacted to the situation, whatever it was, in the same way. It's no wonder those men didn't stick around. I was walking straight into the trap, hands aloft in surrender. *It's a fair cop. Let's get it over with. I'm no different from her.*

"I'm sick of guys telling me how their ex-wife is a crazy jealous narcissist and they don't speak. Harry is still friends with his last partner even though she ended up getting back with *her* ex. He could be really bitter about it, but I think the fact he can resist shows that he has some sort of maturity. He can end a relationship with someone without things getting out of hand. It's so important for the kids."

There was silence while Maya and Sally digested this. Sally had no contact with her brother, and her boyfriend had way too much contact with his wife. Maya, in contrast, had practically no contact with her own husband. Neither of them knew whether I was right or wrong. They managed their lives surrounded by frostiness and had never known anything else.

My perspective on marriage and divorce was more extreme. I remembered the day my father left my mother, the first day of twenty years of vile acrimony. I was away at university but my brother, who still lived at home at the time, lost his whole family at once. He came home one evening to find our father missing and our mother collapsed over an untouched plate of food. After their divorce, my parents never communicated again. Now, twenty years later, my father had Alzheimer's and couldn't speak to anybody if he wanted to. If my mother had ever imagined reconciliation, that dream was over; if retribution, then she had had her way. Their divorce was brutal and costly, leaving scars which left their mark in turn on my brother and me, like a marker pen going through to the next page.

So that's why getting on with exes is a priority of mine.

There were other plus points about Harry that I was keen to share, and perhaps hadn't elaborated on to Sally the previous evening as fully as I could have, so I carried on, as my captive audience desperately wracked their brains for an alternative conversation topic.

"Another thing about him was that he phoned me straightaway rather than days of texting."

I told them about the morning after we first connected on Tinder. I was walking down the railway path with the dog and he called me, told me who he was, what he wanted, and put all his cards on the table. I tried to explain to the girls how the conversation had gone.

"I know it sounds weird", he said "but the thing is, I'm not looking for love. I'm solvent. I'm okay. I'm just..."

I think I interrupted him then with something like:

'I know, I get it, you're fine on your own but to meet someone would be the icing on the cake.'

"You're finishing each others' sentences already, ha!" said Maya.

"Or rescuing him," added Sally. We regularly accused each other of being rescuers. Once our mission had been completed, our newly healed partner would soon be on his way, leaving us puzzled and lonely once again.

"And the thing is, of course, what he said was all bullshit." I made them stop in their tracks, which didn't matter since we were probably walking in circles by this point.

"What do you mean?" Two pairs of eyes frowned at me with incomprehension.

"I mean, when he says *I'm not looking for love and I'm okay on my own*, I just infer that he is not okay on his own and definitely looking for love."

"How do you get to that?" Sally looked baffled.

"I don't know. I just feel that whatever people come out with, you know, first off, it's to counteract the truth. I don't mean all the time, I just mean as a first announcement, a declaration of who you are. That is always going to be a projection of what you think you should be, rather than who you really are. Especially if you're a man. So much more pressure to be a man."

"So you're saying he's a liar? Or all men are liars?" Maya was not getting my point, not understanding that we have a habit of saying things to convince ourselves they are true.

Sally didn't get it either.

"Oh my God Rach, doesn't that make it a bit difficult – working out the truth?" she asked. "I mean where does it stop? Do you just assume the opposite of everything? And if so, that means he's broke anyway, because he said he's solvent."

They had a point. I just knew that he wasn't being honest about not wanting love. Everyone wants to be loved.

"There was another thing that was weird though." I hadn't been meaning to tell them but I was there now. "We were talking about personality disorders. Actually, we were talking about personalities in general to start with. We did the Myers Briggs personality test and he came out with the same result as me."

"Great, so you're twins now," said Sally. "Incredible. Did he show you his workings?"

There was more. "And then he said there's this test for psychopaths."

"Psychopaths?" They both stopped again and looked at me with even more astonishment. "What the...?"

"Apparently there was a documentary about it, then he looked it up out of curiosity and did the test and scored – a high score."

"What? Are you serious?"

"The thing is, that's just another example of him being the opposite. He is no way a psychopath."

"But why would he say he was?" asked Sally. "I mean, I get the point of pretending to be solvent and independent, but why would anyone say they were a psychopath?"

"I don't know. Maybe it's a test?"

"To see how stupid you are?" Sally said. "Seriously, did he say he was a psychopath?" She had stopped properly now and was looking at me with eyes that demanded the truth.

"Yes, but he's not."

"Oh Jesus!" It was Maya's turn to interject. "How can you possibly know? What if it's true, all of it?"

"I'll be fine. I'm a big girl. I can look after myself, and if I thought for a second it was true, I wouldn't be seeing him again."

"You're seeing him *again*?" repeated Maya, reminding me of everyone I had ever met whose mission it was to throw water on my fire.

I didn't tell them he had sent me the link to the Psycho Killer video on YouTube. They wouldn't have understood that it had just become a joke between us now. And I was used to other people's cynicism when it came to online dating. There were the ones who were either coupled up and had never needed to indulge, and those who had thrown the towel in and resigned themselves to singledom. In either case, they couldn't hope to see things from my point of view. Maya wasn't the first. The first person who had tried to lift the scales from my eyes was Isabel Taylor, two weeks earlier...

CHAPTER 4

The box under my bed

It was a couple of weeks after I had first swiped right on Harry. There had been the conversation on the railway path, then a stream of daily WhatsApps and YouTube links, emoji hearts and phone calls that lasted deep into the night, his declaration of love. He eventually suggested we meet up on the next Friday night. Then, that morning, he sent me a text cancelling the date, cutting and pasting a message from his mum onto a WhatsApp to me preceded by the words *"I can't believe I forgot about this!"* The message read:

"The table is booked for 7.30. Can you do me a favour and pick up Brian and Angela on your way?"

It was his mother and stepfather's wedding anniversary dinner. He was mortified at having messed up and begged my forgiveness, asking if we could meet on Sunday instead. I was touched by his apology as well as by the fact he had such a good relationship with his parents that he had been invited out to a celebration of their marriage. It made me feel grateful and safe. I was fine with it. We rescheduled for Sunday. And that's why I ended up going out for dinner with Isabel on the Friday.

Isabel won't mind me saying she has had her fair share of nutters. Her father, who suffered from serious clinical depression, spent years staring at a wall, while her mother fussed around him, attending to his every imagined need and getting precisely no reaction. He stayed like that until the day he died. The effect of her mother's behaviour was to normalise neglect and create an expectation of nothing when it came to relationships. And that is exactly what Isabel found in a husband, an abusive bully only interested in running her down, acquiring ostentatious material possessions and shirking his parental obligations. She was committed to sparing other women the same fate.

"Let's see him then." She reached over for my phone, where I was scrolling through my Tinder matches to find Harry Dawson. I handed it over and watched her face relax into blankness as she took in the photos of this man who, as she kept reminding me, had stood me up at the last minute. Isabel had never had anything good to say about swiping left and right to find a boyfriend, and her expression said that he would be no exception.

"Nice dog. Golden retriever?"

"I guess"

"You know what they say, pose with a dog and the women will come running..."

"He's not *with* the dog though." That was an own goal by me. Isabel raised one eyebrow.

"So it's just a stock photo. Hang on, let me google golden retrievers and see what comes up."

"Oh, come on Iz, give the guy a break!"

I topped up our glasses as she put my phone down and picked up her own.

"What did you say his surname was? What does he do again?"

I studied the menu and sipped my wine as she googled his name, his company name, and drew a blank.

"Who is he?" she asked, simply. "He's nowhere. He doesn't exist."

"I know, you can't find him online, I've looked." I admitted. "It's a bit frustrating really. I like to do my research – you know, get one step ahead."

"Frustrating? It's more than frustrating. It's a red flag. I mean *everyone* has some sort of online presence. Ask him what the company is actually called. It must exist under another name."

He texted right back, explaining that there was a complex corporate structure behind his business but gave me some links to click on. He explained that he needed to keep a lot of what he did under the radar. Isabel was unimpressed.

"Tax evasion."

"Avoidance, maybe?" I said, hopefully.

She looked at his photo again.

"He's got a tattoo on his neck. I bet he's been in prison."

"Really? How do you know?"

"Ask him if he's been in prison, go on."

I thought about it but took the roundabout route instead.

When did you get the tattoos?

After coming off the drugs, he replied straightaway.

He'd told me about the Priory. Everyone needs a chance at rehabilitation, and I told Isabel that, but she was shaking her head, so I asked him straight out by text whether he'd ever been in prison. The reply took a minute or so.

I got a community order for fighting.

The story came out. A man had been threatening a woman in a pub. He had gone to her rescue, knocked the guy out. Isabel just shook her head, but Harry needed to explain further.

Don't forget, I used to box.

I wasn't sure how that excused assaulting someone.

"Ah, boxing. Legalised violence" said Isabel, nodding.

While she went to the bathroom, I poured

the rest of the bottle of wine and Harry and I exchanged a series of furious messages.

I can't believe you didn't tell me that!

What do you mean? Do I have to tell you everything?

You have to tell me the important stuff, like having a criminal record.

Well, you know everything now.

Do I? I know you're a violent drug dealer running some business under the radar, probably money laundering, people trafficking, who knows?

I pressed *send* before I could allow myself to rethink.

He replied that it might be an idea not to meet on Sunday, but to "*talk a bit more*" before arranging something. And then came a surge of guilt at my outburst, for jumping to conclusions, throwing insults at him when all he had done was tell me the truth, albeit about a slightly shady past. I had sent him away. I deserved everything I got if this was the way I behaved towards someone who had genuine feelings for me. I was a disgrace.

Sometimes I don't recognise myself. Press the right buttons, put together the right combination of trigger events and I will see an entirely different woman in the mirror from the one who was there yesterday. A demon sits on my shoulder and holds a mask in front of my face, showing me only a hideous distortion of the truth. With no other option to hand, I submit and retreat from life, because I am worth nothing. I know that when someone else feels like this, I don't get it. I just join in the same old judgmental chorus. *How can such a healthy, intelligent, good-looking, successful, kind, popular woman like you possibly have anything to complain about?*

I was impatient with Adam during his mental illness in the last years of our marriage because of the resentment I felt at having had a part of him stolen from me. I blamed him for tampering with my fairy tale life. I thought he should fight harder, resist the darkness, for me. But he wouldn't. I didn't really consider that perhaps he couldn't, and from there I developed a kind of blanket distrust of the word *depression.* From time to time most of us find ourselves in that place, hiding in a corner, waiting for the cloud to pass and for the demon to climb down. None of us is immune to the darkness.

Neither are we always averse to the charms of a good rescuer, and we can fight tooth and nail against the wisest advice. I knew that Isabel wasn't going to hold back. It didn't surprise me that she said absolutely, categorically, that Harry Dawson should be avoided at all costs.

She moved our empty glasses aside and leant forward across the table. Her expression was blank, emotionless.

"Do *not* go out with this man."

I took a deep breath and sat back, because she was invading my space, spoiling my fun. “Okay, I get why you say that. Let me think.”

She sat back now too, took a sip of wine. I blinked, scratched around for something different to talk about.

“You’re not coming away with us this weekend then?”

“No. Got lots on here.”

“Really? It’s not like you to miss a party.”

“It’s a couples’ retreat isn’t it? Like that film. Can’t imagine anything worse.”

“I’m not in a couple.”

“Not yet.” She raised her eyebrows, glanced around for the waitress and mouthed *can we have the bill please?*

“Maddie’s not in a couple, and Simon’s probably not going. He never goes to things.”

“Maddie's way too enthusiastic for me. Exhausting just thinking about her.”

“That’s a good thing isn’t it? We like a bit of enthusiasm.”

Isabel nodded, pursed her lips. “Up to a point, we do. And you know her way better than I do. Just sometimes it feels a little… I don’t know. Can it be real? Is life really that exciting?”

I thought for a second. “No, not necessarily, but nothing wrong with acting as if it is. Fake it till you make it and all that?"

"Talking of faking it..." She glanced at my phone, where another message had just popped up from Harry. "Why him? How did it start?"

"He looked safe, I suppose." The words came out before I could stop them.

"Safe? Are you sure about that?"

"It's what they look like that you go for when you swipe right. Nothing else to go on except a few random clichés like "I love to travel" and "Not looking for hook-ups", which is usually a lie by the way. Harry looked different. He looked as if he'd look after me."

"Do you need looking after?"

The question hung in the air, unanswered. I was feeling the amputated limb itching again. I had told her about it before and Isabel knew what I meant, but was pragmatic about the procedure, and after hers, which she saw as a key to freedom rather than the loss of safety, she had chosen a different path.

Isabel needed her independence. I was afraid of it. I might not have needed looking after, but I needed, or wanted, a prosthetic husband to step in for the one I'd had removed.

The bill arrived on a saucer with some confectionery wrapped in green shiny paper. Isabel pulled it from under them with the dexterity of a children's party magician and pushed the saucer towards me.

"I'll get this."

I protested weakly , but she held up her hand. "Actually, there is something you can do for me, in return, if you like."

"You name it." I looked straight at her, then felt the joy seep out of my soul as her face clouded.

"Don't meet this man. Find someone as good as you. As clever, funny, kind as you."

She was describing herself, but she was never going to let me turn it back on her.

"Okay but where?"

"I have no idea, and I know you will do what you want to do. But please, please be careful."

And I put her advice in a box under my bed, promising to take it one day, and she saw me do that and just gave me a knowing look that had the wisdom of the world behind it.

When I look at the messages that Harry and I exchanged during that evening while I was out with Isabel, it's a wonder we ever met up at all. It's even more surprising that he was able to spend so much time on his phone while out for dinner with his parents for their anniversary, but I didn't think of that. Not until many weeks later. Things still occur to me now, little things that don't add up, and I wake up in a sweat, my heart pumping, getting ready to run.

How we got to the point of meeting up, how

we climbed out of the ditch that our wayward vehicle had steered drunkenly into, is a story for the psychiatric profession. I don't know how he did it, but over the next two weeks, several hundred texts and phone calls later, he had me back where we wanted me. Tattoos, rehab and community service were worn like battle scars, and if he was working under the radar, then the less I knew about it the better.

And Isabel's words were still locked away as we trudged through the forests of Dorset three weeks later.

CHAPTER 5

We'll have our time

"I think we're lost."

We had turned off the path of Danger of Death and were walking through an open field. It was looking less and less like the idyll where we had begun our morning stroll, and the sun was still showing no sign of breaking through the cloud.

I nodded towards a figure in the distance. "We need to ask this guy the way back. I'm sure this isn't it."

"Ah, that must be your gut feeling again", said Sally.

A jolly rambler with a ruddy face and bright eyes was walking towards us, and guessing we were lost, which wasn't hard, proceeded to point us back to the road. We were heading almost in the right direction after all. The girls gave me a look that said *I told you so.*

"There are a few cows up ahead," he added, "if you don't mind cows"

I liked the way he used "if" as if to say the cows would go away if we did mind.

I don't mind cows at all, and neither did the others, in theory, but then cows are cows and bulls are bulls, and this friendly rambler hadn't conducted a full assessment of the situation. As we rounded the corner to make our way towards the road, we came across what I assessed at first glance to be three hungry bullocks, fully equipped with killer horns and attitude. Indiana Jones (me) came into her element, sheltering town mouse Maya from imminent carnage, while country mouse Sally stepped boldly ahead with a big stick which she planned to wave around in the event of an attack. It was the most exciting thing that happened to us all day, and I made sure that we kept up the whole "face to face with a herd of bulls" side of the story rather than admitting that some cattle were just grazing by the roadside minding their own business. We needed to be labelled as heroes, not just lost and late.

It was probably the most delicious cold beer ever that I gulped down when we finally set foot in the village café two hours later. Jess and the others had been there for ages and were halfway through unfeasibly large doorstep sandwiches. They cheered our arrival, Maddy leapt to her feet and hugged us one by one, chattering about how she *knew* it wasn't a short cut and that we should have taken the road as they had. I wasn't so sure.

Something about huge physical exertion, thirst and the reward of cold bubbles, combine to bring happiness to a whole new level. We felt doubly entitled to celebrate, and James had just the thing. It was birthday banquet and quiz night at Highfield Manor.

Caro looked on with pride as her husband read out the questions, beaming at his innate ability to deal with the drunkest of hecklers. He knows exactly how many times to repeat the question before saying "tough it's too late, hand in your papers," and I am just grateful that quizzes are a team sport With my hard-won degree and PGCE behind me, I still can't recognise the face of my own prime minister on the picture round. There's a name for this inability to see things properly that I can't recall. But Caro's team had no sympathy as they roared and fist-pumped their way to victory.

And it wasn't only quiz night, but the night of swaying lines of tipsy women slumped over their pavlova, whose renditions of *Wuthering Heights* would soon be being used for the torture of terrorists. With my stream of texts, photos and videos, Harry was getting a feel for the kind of girl I was. We talked for an hour on the phone that night. I told him about the walk, the tanks, the cows, the beer, and how he was the focus of everyone's curiosity, but I didn't relay the psychopath conversation because that was all behind us. I had met him, looked into his eyes and seen the man who was going to make everything right.

"Come down tomorrow." It was an invitation offered in the rosy glow of Malbec. He was the missing piece of my puzzle of love.

"To Dorset?"

"Yes, come down for Sunday. I want you to be here. Come down on the new motorbike."

"I'd love to - but do you think it would be okay with everyone else?"

"Yes, they think so."

"You've asked them?"

"Absolutely," I lied, feeling too stupid to admit the truth, and having no idea why I'd asked him.

"You sure they meant it?" His shyness tugged at my heart, made me all the keener to bring him into the fold.

"Yes absolutely. They want to meet you." I had to go on, once I'd started.

"Check I'm not a psychopath you mean?"

"Probably." I didn't like that he kept bringing that up.

We decided to talk again in the morning, by which time I had changed my mind. Apart from the fact that I'd have to run it by the birthday guests, it had occurred to me that Harry's arrival could cause upheaval in the group dynamic that I would feel responsible for, and I didn't want to be responsible for anything. I just told him, tentatively, that Monday might be better. It was only a couple of us staying on the last night, so it made sense to have a quieter time. Our first real date, after all. To my relief he was okay with that. I think that was yet another thing that won me over – a man who is okay with me changing my mind.

"We'll have our time," was all he said.

CHAPTER 6

Ghost mode

The weekenders were hoarse, exhausted, alcohol poisoned and ready to leave, but dragged themselves out the next morning for hearty clifftop walks and sea air. I escaped to my room in the afternoon and spent most of it chatting to Harry on WhatsApp. He had looked at train timetables. He was coming down the next day. I couldn't even nap properly I was so excited.

We ate like kings that night, drank like alcoholics, danced like the drunk parents we were. Our only source of music was a Bluetooth speaker, a thoughtful present for Caro from Maddie whose need to keep moving ensured that we weren't going to go very long without a boogie. But having failed to work out that the volume was controllable from the phone handset we were only able to dance one at a time with the speaker glued to one ear. Maya had the bright idea of getting a louder sound by putting the speaker in a saucepan, but whichever way you looked at it, it was a very bad silent disco. Anyone looking through the window would have called for the men in white coats.

"You..." Caro slurred, flinging one arm around me and the other around Maddie, "are my besss friends. Love you." She planted smudgy kisses on our cheeks and staggered backwards to the sofa, pulling us down with her and bursting into giggles. Jess perched on the arm and held a glass of water out to Caro.

"This isn't like me, I know, but I have your interests at heart, birthday girl."

Caro waved her away. "I'm just sooooo happy, that you're all here, my besss friends, and I don't want anything to get in the way of our friendship..."

"Drink the water. You've stopped making sense." Jess thrust it in her face but she carried on.

"I don't want anything to get in the way. Especially...." She paused for effect, raising her eyebrows and tilting her head down in the manner of a school mistress peering over her glasses. "Especially.... Not men." She looked at me, head slightly wobbling, then at Maddie, who was furiously trying to change the music which had taken on a rather sombre tone, then accepted the water and drank two sips before setting it back down on the table, precariously balanced half on and half off a coaster. I reached out to adjust it and half-heard Caro's last words before she heaved herself up and let herself be swept into a slow dance with

James. I think she said *"No more silly misunderstandings, girls."*

Harry was waiting online for me and when I read his last message the phone buzzed in response.

"Hey babe, how you doing?" His voice was slightly slurred. I took comfort in the presumption that since I could hear that, I must be stone cold sober myself.

"I'm so happy. It's all been amazing. I have had such a great evening, such a great weekend. I am so lucky. I don't deserve this really." I was almost tearful. I get like that when I'm overwhelmed, feeling the love...

"What do you mean, you don't deserve it?"

"I don't know. I haven't always been the best person I could have been. Caro, she's the one with the birthday, brought it up just now, about me and Maddie having had a bit of a misunderstanding in the past, and I just felt so undeserving suddenly. You make a mistake, and people forgive you, and that's just, well, I'm too lucky."

I was ranting. The drink was talking, but Harry didn't seem to notice, and didn't want to know about the thing with Maddie, which was a relief.

"I'm missing you baby. Only met you once, but feels like we've been together a long time."

"I can't wait to see you tomorrow. Where

have you been tonight?"

"What do you mean? Nowhere." His tone was abrupt. I thought of my father being interrogated by my mother on his whereabouts. I mustn't be like that.

"Just – did you go out, or whatever?" I felt chastised. And now I felt nosey, jealous, over-inquisitive. Drunkenness gave way to sobriety in an instant as I felt the adrenaline rush through my body. Was he seeing someone else?

Harry's tone calmed momentarily, as if he sensed my panic.

"No baby, I've been working."

"How's it going? The work?" I was stumbling now, reaching for safer ground.

"Oh, same old. All good."

"On target?"

"Yes, so far, I think."

"You're up late."

"I'm always up late baby, I told you, remember? I do online share dealing, so it's the markets. Got to stay up late to keep it all rolling."

"Ah. You're a wheeler dealer. I almost forgot."

Why had I not remembered that? Why didn't I remember him telling me about his motorbike accident? I felt as if I was constantly playing catch-up, a forgetful granny being reminded that grandpa was dead and that the corner shop had closed forty years ago. A wave of disquiet washed over me as I thought about my sick father, propped up in his armchair in the day room, folding paper napkins with shaking hands as he asked where his wife was. "I'm right here," Jill would reply, and he'd look at her with fear and incomprehension.

I pushed morbid thoughts away.

“Sorry.” I said. Trying to iron out the rumpled conversation with pacifying words was becoming a habit of mine. But my heartbeat had subsided. I needed to be less jumpy.

“I’m looking forward to seeing you baby.”

“Me too.”

It was a relief to hang up this time. My performance on the phone had been shaky at best. The reviews would be damning. I put it down to nerves but resolved to keep live chat to a minimum and stick to texting if I wasn’t going to make myself look like a paranoid idiot.

After a messy brunch the next morning, Caro and James were waved off by the full cohort, and we trudged back indoors to repair the general devastation, wrap leftovers in cellophane and divide up the remains of the cake between us. Jess and Jason were last to leave in the afternoon, along with Maya, who had been planning on staying an extra night but didn’t fancy playing gooseberry or being murdered in her bed by a psychopath, which was understandable. There was a sombre mood on the drive as we hugged goodbye. They were worried about leaving me alone in a manor house with a strange man I'd met for twenty minutes. I thought that was the most exciting thing imaginable. A WhatsApp check-in group was created. I promised to provide regular updates.

"I've got a better idea." Maya climbed out of the car and pulled out her phone. "It's what I do with my kids. Well, it's what they do, and basically the only way I communicate with them."

She opened up Snapchat, an app I had downloaded out of curiosity but had rarely used, and showed me how to use a map feature I didn't know even existed.

"Because I have enabled it on my phone as well, we can always see where each other is." She opened up the app on her own phone and zoomed in on two miniature versions of us, snuggling together in the middle of a map of Dorset.

"Well that's going to be really useful – knowing which county I'm in," I laughed.

"Oh it goes much more specific than that." She zoomed in further, and there we were, just off Main Street, with the Larder Café just half a mile down the road. I nodded in reluctant admiration. Then Maddie appeared on the same map, a cute blonde avatar with worryingly purple eyelids. "Ta daa," she said.

I zoomed out, and saw Sadie in London, *last*

seen an hour ago at school. I could get used to this, I thought.

"Sadie will have enabled it too. You can't see just anyone, you can't even see your own friends, unless they allow it." Maya was on a roll here, the new technology consultant, the bridge between middle-aged parents and their unwieldy offspring.

"Okay, you got me. That is genius." We said our goodbyes with renewed confidence, and I felt extra safe, a little too safe perhaps, knowing they would be able to follow my every move.

"Just don't go into ghost mode," she called out of the window.

I could imagine what that was.

And the next person I saw that day was Harry.

CHAPTER 7

Flamingo

I have a tendency, despite my acute awareness of it, to take control of situations. I try not to use the phrase "control freak" because firstly it is overused and secondly it has exclusively negative connotations. In my experience, most of us who wear that label have simply lost their ability to trust. We have somehow learnt that leaving things to others to organize just won't do, and I'm thinking mainly about women who have had children and done the bulk of the childcare, on top of their job and organising what remains of their social life. The moment they hand little Felix over to Daddy he will without a shadow of a doubt run into the road, wet his pants and shoot the neighbours' cat. Therefore, we have no choice but to be in charge, of everything, at all times. Then we complain we are too exhausted for anything fun and you can pretty much go straight to divorce, do not pass go, and don't collect £200, just times it by a hundred and hand it over to the lawyer.

I was keen to take some control over the afternoon with Harry before it even started. I had had the marvellous idea of collecting him from the station and driving him blindfold to Monkey World, whereupon we would have the kind of perfect day Lou Reed sang about. I watched him walking down the platform and relished those moments before he saw me. I took in his stature, his ruddy features, the languor of his gait, and allowed myself to imagine being held tight in an embrace that had been so many agonising weeks coming.

He spotted me in the car park just as he was crossing the footbridge, and gave me a wave, silhouetted against the sun. I was leaning against the car, one foot up behind me against the door, looking like some sort of flamingo, holding my phone in my sweaty hands. Phones are like mummies and daddies. Holding our phone, we are holding their hand– it makes us safe, keeps us in touch with the ones who pull the strings, wear the trousers, call the shots. I wondered whether I should run up to him and leap into his arms or wait for him to saunter over to me at his leisure, then I settled for something in between and met him half way, in the middle of the car park where we took centre stage for all to see. Swinging his rucksack over his shoulder, he leaned down and kissed me. My heart leapt with excitement as his lips brushed mine and lingered there a second too long. His arms were around me, holding me close. I breathed in and feltthe scent of his neck fill my lungs. On the outbreath all my tension lifted and my spirit soared with certainty. This was meant to be.

Harry smiled a smile that said he felt the same.

"How about we grab last orders at the pub."

I thought that was a splendid idea. We would be just in time and alcohol would oil the wheels of this unconventional encounter. Monkey world was shelved and never mentioned. I stood at the bar and texted the check-in group while he went to the loo to say it was all fine, and the relief of letting go of the reins flooded through me. I carried our drinks to the table.

“Cheers baby.” He was back before I'd even pressed send. He lifted the Guinness to his lips and gulped thirstily.

“Texting already?”

I turned the phone over. “No, that can wait. You were quick!”

“Cheers,” he said again. "God that's good."

“Thanks for coming down,” I said.

“The pleasure is all mine. How are you feeling?” He sat down opposite me at the table.

“I'm okay. I'm more than okay. How was the journey?”

“Long, hot, but I got some work done. It's all good.” He took another swig. “God, that really does hit the spot. I'm a bit hungover.”

"Hungover? I thought...."

He looked surprised. "I don't think you can talk, can you? I've seen the videos, remember..."

I did remember sending him the three-man version of Oops Upside your Head, with barely audible soundtrack. He had a point.

"What did you drink?" I asked him.

"Oh, some wine, and a friend came round, and then we had some lemon vodka, at least I think it was lemon."

"Oh, so happy hair of the dog then." We clinked glasses.

And of course I was actually wondering *which friend?* And why he hadn't mentioned it last night on the phone? But you don't ask, in case you look jealous, and we had vowed that we would never be jealous, like Craig had been.

I talked about me, then he talked about him. I was confused about the chronology and made him tell me again where he'd lived and when, how the partners and children fitted into his roaming life, how he had split up with them, how his relationships were now with the exes, with the kids. He padded out the gaps in my knowledge of him so I could tell it back to him almost perfectly. I felt like a spy in training, adopting a new identity, practising a false narrative to deliver to my captors in case of discovery and torture. He stopped at the last break-up, leaving ten years of occasional dating to my imagination. I inferred that no woman had made the grade or made enough of an impression to warrant talking about. I wasn't curious enough to ask about previous lovers, and was grateful that we slipped the thorny subject of sex with other partners into sanitised packages of heavily censored information.

"What do you want to do?" I checked the time on my phone. At two thirty, the night was very young, in fact several hours off yet. He smiled inquiringly at my question, making me blush, then steered the conversation away from where both our minds were.

"How about we go back to the house, I dump my stuff and get changed and we go for a walk?"

"Sounds like a plan." I was letting him take the lead. It was a new feeling, and a good one.

"We can take a bottle of wine, go and sit in a field somewhere."

I was happy to let it play out. The sun had suddenly come out of hiding to beam down its celestial approval, for the first time in two days.

My phone rang as we drove up to the front door, and I took the call while letting Harry in. He motioned for permission to explore, and I stepped into the garden to talk. It was Adam, asking about various things to do with the kids, telling me our fifteen-year-old son had come back drunk on gin from a party the night before. Adam said he just wanted to let me know so that I could reinforce the no-boozing message on my return. Either that, or he was instinctively calling me to check I was okay.

He has always had a bit of a sixth sense about me being with other men. He has had his own non-stop stream of post-divorce girlfriends, but I always felt the tension between us when it came to any new partner of mine. It sparked a sense of shame and guilt in me, which I knew to be my own, not his responsibility. We are in charge of our emotional reactions to others, I am told by every single book I read on the subject. If I explored my guilt I would probably find it rooted in fear, fear I'd failed, done the wrong thing, that I'd hurt him, should have tried harder, when the reality of it was we had squeezed every drop out of our marriage until there was nothing left, dragged it from therapy room sofa to the lawyer's boardroom table, only to have it confirmed by decree that it was long dead, and that this was nobody's fault.

I turned back to the house, to see Harry emerging from the front door holding a glass of white wine. I hung up the phone and must have looked slightly too long at his glass because he said

"What's the matter? Is it the wine?"

He knew.

"Yes." I just said it, hesitantly, but I said it. "Yes, it's the wine."

"I'm not Craig."

"I know you're not."

At that moment, he was everything I couldn't bear about Craig. Until that moment, I had brushed aside my instinct that his drinking went beyond the limits of the "socially acceptable". One Monday afternoon he had rung me from a bar, after a meeting with a client, and by the end of our conversation, he seemed to be most of the way through a bottle of wine. His voice had begun to slur, but I was too busy taking it all in. The words, I'm falling for you babe, whether slurred or not, produced a ripple of delicious excitement through my body. The fact was that the more he drank, the more he was in love with me, which is all I wanted, or so I thought.

He looked at me searchingly, then said "Let's go for a walk then."

Aside from the correlation between alcohol and declarations of love, I was trying to normalise the parts of Harry that unsettled me, because I wanted to believe him. If he was real, then I was wonderful, and there was a gaping hole in my self-esteem that needed that assurance. I was playing out a familiar pattern, dancing around waiting for his approval. He probably spotted me a mile off.

The best way to normalise someone else's drinking is to drink with them. Two alcoholics together can easily rationalise the activity for each other to the point that they become reliant on each other facilitating it. I packed a rucksack with a bottle of wine and two glasses and a bag of Doritos, put on my trainers and sunglasses and watched Harry tie his shoelaces meticulously. I watched him for a second, puzzled that someone could take such pains to get each loop exactly the right size, double knotting it over the top for extra security. He caught my eye.

"You alright babe?" That was to become the chorus in the soundtrack to our relationship, but had already changed its tone from a carefree "orr-right?" to something more concerned, more laden with meaning I couldn't quite capture.

If you go for a walk with someone you don't know, in a place you don't know, it's a chance to find things out about each other, not just in conversation, but in the way someone walks, where they want to get to, the landmarks they point out, the route they take. It's a micro-life journey. Harry and I didn't take any paths at any point. It was a wild and random walk. After a few minutes, we came to a gate into the next field that said Private Property, KEEP OUT. I know I had been down a path two days earlier that said danger of death, but that was a public footpath, and the military must have to follow public safety rules for insurance purposes, so the danger was in all likelihood minimal. But to me, KEEP OUT means KEEP OUT. Makes me think of Peter Rabbit and Mr McGregor. Harry just laughed and looked at me with incomprehension.

“You’re so funny. What are you scared of?”

“I don’t know. Being shot?”

“You won’t get shot. People do this all the time.”

“How do you know?”

“Look, it’s a field of sheep. Now if we came piling in with a pack of mad dogs that would be another matter, but we’re not doing any harm, we’re just walking through. How bad can it be?”

I agreed to do it, because it was the only way forward anyway, and the hills beyond looked too enticing. As we neared the other side, he gave me a squeeze.

“You see? It wasn’t so bad was it?”

I shook my head and let out the breath I'd been holding. I felt small, scared, naïve, but exhilarated.

“Shall we aim for that tree over there?”

I followed his pointing finger. A lonely oak stood in a fallow field, strangely out of place, stark against the horizon. I looked to the right where a path led up a hill to an invisible other world. I wanted to see what other world it was.

“Can’t we go a bit further up?”

He didn’t take much persuading. He knew his own mind but was easy about having his plans adjusted. We weren’t disappointed. The higher we climbed, the more of this other world, this middle earth, revealed itself. Like the sun suddenly emerging, this was another Truman Show set thrown together at the last minute to meet our change of plan. I could imagine the directors putting the last stone in place just as we rounded the corner. It looked brand new. Strange structures, of different shapes and sizes, colours and materials, were scattered about the grass. Cuboids, cubes, indefinable forms, made of wood, stones, grass, like a sparse futuristic graveyard. Across the summit of the hill, three giant tombs, each topped with a haystack, like double ended sunbeds, stood squarely against the sky.

"Horse jumps." Sally would have loved it here. I stopped to take photos with my phone and noticed my battery was dying.

We made our way towards the biggest one, climbed on top and settled ourselves at each end, head against haystack, legs stretched out towards each other. Harry poured the wine and handed me a glass. It was only four thirty. I relished the decadence of the scene and felt a warmth around me that was more than the heat of the sun.

"I knew you'd ask me to come down." His eyes looked right into my mind and pulled out truths I couldn't hide.

"Did you? I didn't," I lied again.

"Honestly? I think you knew you'd ask, and you knew I'd say yes."

"I'm glad you did."

We talked about who we were, what we wanted, described our fantasy homes, a sprawling farmhouse overlooking the lush valleys of the Dordogne (me), a Greek olive plantation with all profits going to the local villagers (him). We went back over our initial conversations, each remembering something the other had forgotten, raking over the detail to find the moments where we had moved on, become closer, made this inevitable, the moment when he knew he was falling for me, and when he realised, or we both did, that we were meant to be together.

My phone beeped. The WhatsApp / Snapchat group was wondering what I was doing in a field two miles from the house. I reassured them that all was good, as good as it gets. I told Harry and he said he was just glad that my friends knew I was safe.

I swapped glasses with him when he had finished his. I sank back into my haystack and soaked up the last rays of this sunshine that had arrived especially for us. We took a selfie on my phone just before the battery died. I didn't tell him it had died though. I must have had a sense that something wasn't quite right.

We wandered back, hand in hand, as the sun sank lower in the sky, and watched it set from a bench in the garden with another bottle of wine. We kissed. He smelt right, and I let him share my four-poster, as if that was ever in doubt. I wanted him near me, his weight on top of me, his limbs intertwined with mine. Away from the judging eyes of friends, the needs of my family and the responsibilities of work, I was free to be myself. A tidal wave of excitement and anticipation rushed through me as he explored my body with gentle hands. I held my breath in case it broke the spell.

"Have you fallen for me yet babe?"

I snuggled into his warmth as he wrapped his arms tightly around me. There is a huge release of tension when you bury your face in that place where chest meets shoulder. It must be the pheromones or something that are at their optimum level just there. I drank in his scent, felt his heart beating against mine. I didn't have to say anything in reply.

"It's okay, I know," he said.

CHAPTER 8

Sand nest

Harry was an early riser, and I mean early. I was woken by tea in bed at six, and he played me music on his phone while I luxuriated in a hot bubble bath. I could have stayed there all day, but check-out time was ten o'clock and we had decided on a day at the beach. We packed our bags and he carried them downstairs, checking under the bed and in the drawers, the sort of thing that parents do for children but nobody does for parents. He found and cooked bacon and eggs that we ate at the table in the garden. Belinda arrived to begin the clear-up, and he charmed her with his smile and easy chat, asking if by any chance the house was free for any weeks over the rest of the summer. It was. A week in August was available at a discount rate if we could take it then and there.

"I'll book it for you baby, for your birthday present," said Harry when she was out of the room.

"You can't do that. It's too expensive."

"It's not that much. A couple of grand."

"Really? You don't think a couple of grand is much?"

"You could come here with the kids, even Adam, have some time all together. I could come at the end of the week, and we could have our time." Our time. It was planned. It was definite. He wasn't running away.

When my father left my mother for another woman she was fifty years old. He had been her only partner for thirty years, and had chosen to wait until my brother and I were on the point of leaving home, which only intensified her pain. She was destroyed, bereft, set adrift on uncharted waters and unable to do more than keep herself alive. Inside I was drawing my own subconscious conclusions: *Men have power over women. A woman, however intelligent and educated, is nothing without a man and will be destroyed if he leaves. He will leave for someone younger, the opposite of me. I have been abandoned by him too because I am of no more use to him. Perhaps I am of no more use to the world."*

As the years went by, I chose partners whose departure wouldn't matter, boyfriends I didn't love, men I felt superior to, who could walk away and leave no scars on me. It was just a sticking plaster over a wound. From time to time the plaster fell off, and I found another one. My married life was a fluffy bunny dream. I chose the perfect partner, the perfect father for my children, who would never leave, never change. I was a princess, and princesses didn't get divorced. Adam was the superplaster. His existence told me that things could be different.

The failure of my marriage is like a page ripped out of me, forcing me to confront the demons that had taken up residence in my head and my heart. Adam didn't abandon me in the traditional way. He showed me there were other options available when it came to splitting up. *50 ways to leave your lover...* At the risk of sounding fatalistic again, my divorce was meant to be. I had lessons to learn about other types of pain.

Harry might have understood my fear of loss. Or he might have read a book by Russell Brand on pulling women, or he might just be the same as me, because he was my match, my mind-reader, my soul brother. Because later that day as we lay in the dunes at Studland Bay, he asked me how I saw the future. I talked about my career, my home, my kids, but he didn't mean that peripheral stuff. He sat up and leaned over me on one elbow.

"What about us babe? Where do you see us?"

I felt too awkward to give a straight answer. To paint a picture of wedded bliss would be insane, and I wasn't ready to make any declarations of intent. I didn't believe he was thinking like this. Men didn't. And I was the last person to inspire commitment in a man. I was in my mid-forties, not skinny or beautiful, not Cassandra the model sipping coffee in bed. He could have anyone he wanted. It couldn't be real that he wanted to be with me long-term. I pulled him towards me and kissed him.

"We'll see."

We lay in each others' arms in a kind of sand nest, playing songs on our phones, soaking up the heat, hiding from the wind, then when we started to feel burnt, got up and wandered along the beach and paddled in the freezing sea. He went deeper, up to his knees, splashing water on his arms and neck.

"It's for my psoriasis. The salt is good for it." The lesions on his calves looked painful, made him vulnerable, made me want to look after him.

"Do you have medication for it?"

"I have to inject once a month. It's worse now, because I missed a day. It's not normally this bad."

I had been oblivious to his skin condition, just as I was to his protruding stomach, his teeth damaged by the microphone in his motorcycle helmet smashing into them when he was hit by a drunk driver. When someone comes along who wants you, it's easy to overlook everything else. Like Sally said, I was covering up failure, slapping new wallpaper straight on top of old, forcing my unremarkable life into a Cinderella story.

We talked about the accident. He showed me a photo of the bike he had on order to replace the one that was a write-off. The Kawasaki he had bought a few days ago was to tide him over until the new shiny Ducati arrived. Excess wealth is the enemy of patience, and Harry could afford not to delay his gratification, but I was surprised he wanted to get back on the road so soon after the accident.

"I'm a petrol head baby. Bikes and cars. Love them. Love the speed."

I know as much about cars and bikes as I do about quantum physics. The names Mercedes and Ducati rang bells with me, as did Rolex and Ray Ban, but none of it did anything more than skim over the surface. I was never interested in a glitzy life. Just someone to be with me as an equal, intellectually, financially, emotionally.

Then he said that his phone had been buzzing constantly in his pocket and excused himself, saying he should check his messages. His house was on the rental market and he was anxious to find out whether the day's viewings had yielded any good news. I went into the café to get us some drinks. On my return, he was grinning all over his face. He kissed me on the lips.

"Two offers!"

"On your house?"

"Yes. Two families both want it."

"So – you're going to a bidding war? Who's the agent?"

He hesitated for a second, as if distrusting my motives for asking, or maybe trying to remember their name. "Grants. They think they can get four and a half grand."

"A month? For a four bed house?"

He frowned at me slightly, as if I'd let him down. "It's in a great location, near the schools and the station, they are in huge demand. And my stepfather is mates with the guy who owns the agency, so it was off the record, and I got a better deal."

Had I spoken out of turn in doubting the rental income potential of a house in Surrey? When you watch me with men it looks as if I live in fear of them feeling emasculated. I have no idea what I am afraid of there, or where I have witnessed the wrath of challenged manhood, but that's what was happening again. I was cringing inwardly at my own words as I said them.

"Wow well done, that's brilliant! But where will you live?"

"Putney hopefully. That's the plan. Or Spain."

"Spain?"

"I must have told you about that. Costa Blanca. Just a small place but perfect for the beach and the nightlife. Views over the Med. I've got to go out there anyway to do some notary stuff, put it into the kids' names for tax reasons. All very dull really."

I felt a rush of abandonment. I wanted to say *don't go to Spain. I need you here,* but I said, "Sounds like a plan, whatever works out." And gave him a hug. "It's all looking good for you Harry. And the app sounds so brilliant. You're going to make your fortune."

"Well I'm not counting on anything yet, but if it works it will be massive."

We clinked our bottles and drank to the future, whatever it held. He caught my eye then a second later looked away, leaned back against the table and stretched his legs.

I held the icy bottle against my cheek and relished the relief it brought.

"So your company name Hasam – I'm guessing that is Harry and Sam?"

"Yes he was the guy I set it up with originally."

"I'm a great detective. I knew it."

"You're a great kisser," he said, leaning over and brushing his lips against mine.

"Yeah I know that too."

We sipped cold beers, hiding in the shade of an umbrella now that our sunburn was beginning to take hold. He held my hand, touched my face, looked right into my heart.

Then the phone buzzed in his pocket again. He extricated himself, stood up and said "Harry" with the authority of one who has no need to elaborate. I would offer people my full name, and more often than not would at least have a go at working out who was calling so that I could address them as well. I admired his swagger, wanted to be like him, envied his not needing to please anyone.

"Yeah, that all sounds fine. Can I call you back a bit later? I'm just with my..." he motioned to me and shrugged his shoulders, grinning and questioning, "....girlfriend?"

I blushed, wanting it but not wanting it. When he hung up, he asked me formally, like a proposal. I was typing a quick check in to the girls, who hadn't seen my last one, I noted.

"So, I didn't know what to call you..." He paused, raised his eyebrows in that schoolboy manner I was beginning to pick up on. "*Would* you like to be my girlfriend?"

I put down my phone and hesitated much too long, which sounds surprising, because in my mind I was already there, living the dream. But the reality was that I didn't trust myself to bring that dream into my life. I would be bringing it straight into the path of my self-sabotage, making it real would make it unreal. Men leave women. Men leave me. If we were together it would be just a question of time before he knew me better and saw me for the imposter I was.

"It depends what you mean by girlfriend."

"What do you think it means?"

Somehow, we came to an agreement that the definition of our relationship was not dating other people, not swiping left or right on dating apps. We drank to it. He composed a message to send to the girls he was still chatting to on Tinder. I never saw him send it. But I didn't need to.

I was on the coffee by now because of driving. I had paid for the beers, and now the coffees. It wasn't relevant at the time, but it is now, not just because of how things turned out, but because it has taught me something. I can see that I pay for things to smooth the path to something I need. His wallet was in the car. I could have let him go and get it, but that would have interrupted the flow, and if you lose the flow, you risk falling off the trajectory, and that's abandonment for me. I couldn't risk that, but I should have. I should have trusted in the flow returning, because a flow that is so easily lost isn't a flow worth having.

He drove my car back to London in the end. I fall asleep easily in cars and the sun and the wind, as well as the early start were beginning to take their toll. I struggled to keep my eyes open, yet forced them awake, unused to being driven, conscious that he had drunk more than me, that I hadn't even known him a day, had no proof he even had a licence. Ridiculous worries, but they were there, circling like flies. I dozed to the sound of the radio, giving in, letting it all go on around me, fighting sleep until I had no more fight in me.

I wanted to drop him at his house (partly so I could see it, put him in context and tick a box somewhere) but he had promised to visit his friends Neil and Cass in Farnham on the way back. My stomach lurched momentarily. Cassandra the lustrous-haired model was actually real. My vision of her must have been a premonition. I fought the thought and it subsided as Harry explained the background, oblivious. They were going through a rough time and Cass wanted to move out but couldn't afford to, so Harry was offering her cash to help her make a new start. The next day he told me she wouldn't take the money. It seemed she and Neil were going to try again to make things work. But at least the money was there if she needed it. Can't say fairer than that. I put that on the pile with his offer of my week in Dorset, and concluded that if he was this generous, then there was even more wealth to manage than I had first thought.

I would like to say again, now, that money doesn't matter to me, but if I was impressed by his generosity, then that can't be true. It's like I said on the walk with Maya and Sally, if you are at pains to assert something, then maybe the opposite is true, and maybe at some level I want to be with a rich man. Maybe money has connections with safety. My father spent huge amounts of money on his mistresses. Having money spent on you must mean you are loved.

The sun was setting on our second day together as we pulled into the empty station car park. Neil and Cass lived around the corner and it was the easiest place to drop him without losing my way back to the A3. That's what he told me, and I had no real reason to disbelieve him. It was our third station in as many days.

There was no-one about. He kissed me on the lips and walked away, rucksack on his back, and I climbed into the driver's seat, for the last leg of my journey back to reality.

CHAPTER 9

Neither the time nor the place

Maya had left three messages on the WhatsApp group. Was I okay or had I been murdered in my bed? Was I back yet? How had it been? Sally had sent a few texts, impatiently demanding an update, and to know I was still alive. What was with all these people worrying about nothing? I reassured them both that I was home, and that they could check their app to prove it.

Can I pop round? Or is it too late? replied Maya straightaway.

No, come round, it's fine.

The children and the dog were still at Adam's. I was grateful for the slow transition back to my other life, my life from before the weekend which now had a new sheen to it. The house was chilly, the cat unsettled. Another bulb had gone in the chandelier, which gave off a sad half-light as I sank into the sofa. I reached for my phone to check my emails. Anxious parents were asking whether I was back yet, and would I be able to fit in a session with Connor, Max, Alex one evening this week...? There was a long message from Adam about his limited availability to have the children over the next few weeks. My eyes flicked over the words that jumped out at me *work..... travelling ..... problem.... busy* and half absorbed them. There was a mutual understanding between us that he wouldn't be upfront about when he was away with Sophie. I must have made it clear on some drunk occasion or other that it wasn't the done thing to "parade" your new girlfriend in front of your ex-wife, not that Adam would have done anything of the sort. But you can phrase things a certain way and they take on a whole new look. I did that to make my friends feel sorry for me, take me under their wing and point the finger back at the bad husband who abandoned me.

I looked back at WhatsApp. Nothing from Harry, just my face staring back at me from his profile picture.

"Never put a woman in my status picture before."

Those had been his words just before he got out of the car. A token of his commitment to me, and a sign that this was different, better, worth making changes for. I needn't worry. Everyone would know about me now.

The doorbell rang and the cat jumped off my lap in anticipation. Maya bustled in with crisps and a bottle of elderflower fizz.

"I thought maybe a night off the booze?"

"You thought right." I took the offerings and gave her half a hug with my free arm.

"Well that was a fun weekend. I'm still recovering. My liver is not thanking me for the half bottle of port I managed to pour into it on Saturday night.

"I don't think sticking to the red wine did me any favours. My students haven't had the best lessons this week, to be fair."

"No refunds for hangovers Rach. Or you'd never make a profit." She nudged me and threw her head back in a Maddie-like cackle. I told her so.

"Oh no, don't say it's infectious. What was it with you two, by the way? She seemed upset."

"What do you mean? Did she say something?" My reaction was instinctive, defensive. I thought it was just me that had picked it up, but the sadness in Maddie's eyes when Caro mentioned our "misunderstanding" had not gone unnoticed.

"No she didn't say anything to me at all. She was singing to the radio most of the way home, and texting Chris, who was apparently at some family do with his wife, poor chap. It was Jess that was asking me what was going on. So what is it? Maddie looked as if she'd seen a ghost."

I rolled my glass between my hands, staring at the bubbles, watching them burst and disappear, like fantasies.

"There was something, but it's over. Nothing major and it never gets mentioned. So much water under the bridge."

Maya looked at me quizzically. "No more details?"

"Nothing else. I don't want to bring things back into the present that are safely buried in the past. Best way of doing that is not talking about them."

"If you say so," she said, looking unconvinced.

"So, what about the mystery man? How did it all go? Are you going to see him again?"

My phone was face down on the table. It would buzz if there was a message.

"Yes, I'm definitely going to see him again, but work is busy this week, so not sure when it's going to happen."

"Yours or his?"

"Mine, and I think his too." It occurred to me that we hadn't talked much about the routine of his daily grind. I knew about the business itself, but not about his role in it. I had a vision of him going round cracking the whip until his team of lackeys were sweating blood.

"How is Simon?" I asked.

"Oh I have no idea. I barely see him these days."

"Is he seeing someone else?"

"I wish he was, and then he'd leave us in peace at least."

"You don't mean that"

"No I don't really mean it. I mean, I don't know how I'd actually feel if someone else was managing to enjoy him, bring out the best in him, you know?"

"I know exactly what you mean." When Adam found his first girlfriend after we split up, I was consumed with an irreconcilable jealousy that I couldn't comprehend, until someone pointed out to me *you think she is succeeding where you failed* and that was it. I had to fight that feeling for a long time. Eventually I replaced it with something like *Adam and I have had the best we could have out of each other. There is nothing left. We tried everything.* But the voice telling me that she has won and I have lost is ringing loud and clear in my head. Maya read my mind.

"Is Adam seeing anyone at the moment?"

"Yes, someone from the shopping channel. Sells Liz Earle stuff. Stunning, young, skinny, you name it, she's got it."

"I like Liz Earle. Can she get me some?"

I raised my eyebrows. "No, probably not, Maya. *Please can you get some freebies for my ex-wife's friend.* Can you see him saying that? Can you see me asking him to?"

"Well, at least you've both got someone.

That's good. Makes things a bit more equal."

"Yes, although I'd rather it was more relaxed than some sort of game of catch-up."

"How is Adam, in himself I mean?"

"He's doing okay. I think. I mean, it's a good sign he has a girlfriend I suppose, and his work is going well. I suppose when you think about what he went through, it's amazing how he's turned things around."

"How do you *actually* feel about him seeing other people now?"

She was direct and that was a reason I liked her. There was no skirting around an issue, and she had a knack of pulling needles out of haystacks – in this case a needle I thought was safely hidden in the straw forever.

"It's fine. I'm happy for him. He deserves it."

"Really?" She looked concerned. "Not sure anyone really means that stuff."

My hands were shaking slightly, and I reached for a cushion to clasp in front of me. "Of course. We spent enough years trying to make things work. Time to let someone else have a go."

"It sounds like you're trying to get the lid off a jam jar."

"You know what I mean."

"I do. I totally do. I've definitely had all there is to have from Simon. Just wish he'd go and let someone have a go at taking his lid off."

"You don't mean that. You just said, nobody actually does mean it."

We shared a thoughtful silence.

"I'd probably miss him. Do you miss Adam?"

"I miss the Adam from before."

"Before the darkness...."

"Before the darkness. Although I mainly remember the darkness, and the lead-up, when the lights were dimming and I knew it was coming."

The lights began dimming many months before they were finally extinguished. Adam would leave the house early in the morning and return exhausted after the children had gone to bed. I would be waiting, hot dinner on the stove, the lounge lit by soft lamplight, a bottle of wine and two glasses laid out on the granite worktop of our extended kitchen. *Look at this,* it all said, *look at this and love it and love me and do this for me too.*

Sometimes he came home an hour or so earlier, but only to rush out again to a meeting of school governors or the parish council. If the children asked, I'd tell them what a difficult job he had and that things wouldn't always be like that. Left on my own I would roam my unappreciated surroundings, unable to justify my sadness, when after all he was doing all this for us. He had told me that enough times, sometimes when he leapt out of bed at the first stroke of the alarm. More often than not, I had been lying awake for hours, hoping for the warmth of his arms around me, loving words to remind me who I was to him. But none came.

"This isn't the time or the place", he reprimanded me one morning when I let the tears come. But he never offered me another time or place. He became gradually colder, more disconnected. Sometimes, on a Friday night he might suggest we go to the pub for a drink and I would glimpse the real him, the warm, confident, funny man I'd married, the man who'd made me feel I was the luckiest, safest, most loved girl in the world. Then a weekend packed with children's activities and DIY would put paid to any suggestion of change.

The change came in a way nobody had predicted, when we were on holiday in France. A panic attack in a market square, followed by others, followed by a series of medical investigations for epilepsy and other rational explanations for the way Adam's mind had exploded. He didn't know if his thoughts were about real events or imagined. He lived in a constant state of fear, uncertainty and déjà vu, and the angry distant man became almost overnight, a small frightened boy. Meanwhile ten-year-old Josh found himself stepping in to fill the giant shoes of a father he had only just started getting to know.

Maya had witnessed this from a distance, as an almost neighbour with an impressively practical attitude to life. She had looked after our children while we attended medical appointments, while I visited Adam in hospital. She invited us over for lunch with Simon and their family, keeping our lives going as if nothing had happened, doing everything to reassure our children that they were safe and supported. Her own problems with her marriage, her job, her children, were put on a shelf, to be dusted off and dealt with when we had gone home.

"You were so good to us you know." I said, remembering that. "I don't think you realise how good."

"Don't be silly. You'd have done the same. You might have to, if I have to live with Simon much longer. I'll be in the madhouse too."

"I hope it doesn't come to that."

"You've done a good job Rach. You had to run everything, take over being Daddy as well as Mummy. It can't have been easy with all that responsibility and all the worry about the kids and going to work every day. And the kids have done so well too. Anna loves uni, and Sadie has taken over the eldest-daughter-at-home role like a total natural."

"And the eldest daughter's *bedroom*." It was like a coronation – Anna has gone off to uni, long live her successor in the ensuite... But who could blame her? Rights and privileges are hard won in families, and often unfairly dished out by exhausted parents who are most likely to give in on a first come first served basis. When we first moved to New Malden, Sadie stood in front of me articulating an expertly crafted argument as to why she should be allocated her room of choice, leaving Josh raising his eyes heavenwards and slumping onto the sofa while the decision was made without him. Missing out on her top choice by a small margin to her older sister, who was mid-A levels at the time, Sadie nonetheless secured the promise of a smooth handover scheduled for the very second Anna had left the building on her way to university.

"You've made it so lovely for them. Look at your house. It's warm, it's welcoming. It's like you've just stepped into the breach and not only kept everything going but made it ten times better. It's so full of colour and warmth."

She was being kind. I mean, the place was cosy enough, but the décor and clutter uniquely eclectic. Random glass jars of lentils and rice lined the shelves alongside chipped Le Creuset pots and half-used candles. A tall vase of dusty artificial gladioli stood next to an improbably hardy basil plant. Under the shelves, a sagging wine rack stored not only a fine collection of Lidl Sauvignon Blanc but tubes of tennis balls and sour cream and chive flavour Pringles. On the table there was a half-finished game of Scrabble and a couple of festering mugs of tea. This was me, a bunch of mixed up stuff that somehow worked. Maya read my mind.

"You've made this yours. You've sorted it. Against all odds, when you think about it. You took over running this family and it's been a fantastic success."

I had done some taking over before, first of all in my parents' separation twenty-five years earlier. When Dad left, Mum collapsed, both mentally and physically, leaving me and my brother in charge of everything, including her job. I stepped in to take over her evening class at Brookfields College, teaching law to trainee accountants, and that was where I got my first taste of the world of education. But it wasn't till my early forties that, after failing as a solicitor (my view, probably not a complete fail, but not a massive success) I embarked on a teacher training course. I eventually found my niche in private tuition where, as an overloaded single parent, I found a way of managing the kids and the house (and the dog, let's not forget him) at the same time as earning enough to keep the whole thing rolling along. After his breakdown, the job Adam found when poverty drove him back into the workplace paid a fraction of his salary from the wonder years, so his ability to help out was limited. I needed to earn money.

What I loved most about teaching children was doing everything possible to inspire them before they became disappointed with the world and started working / self-medicating their way into comfortable oblivion. My aspirations for teaching mirrored my expectations in the rest of my life. I was obsessed with getting the best out of everyone.

I just needed to control my instinct to rehabilitate the entire male population, one at a time.

Harry had been in rehab fifteen years before I met him. He had been open during our conversations about being addicted to crack cocaine in a former life as a city trader. I didn't question it, because why would you make that up? But then why would you make up being a psychopath? He was in the Priory with Robbie Williams. We were the solicitor and the crack addict, like one of Aesop's fables, or a modern-day DH Lawrence novel. I was doing what I did best, search and rescue.

"So how did you leave it with Harry?"

"I don't know. We didn't really agree anything."

"But you're going to see him again?"

"Yes, definitely, although…" I felt a momentary rush of fear hit my stomach, like when the swinging boat goes down, and down, and half your insides seem to get left behind at the top.

"What? You've zoned out. What is it?"

"Nothing. It's probably nothing."

"It's never nothing, Rach, you know that."

As I waved her off into the night, Maya

threw me a thumbs-up over her shoulder. Her bike wobbled for a second before she got her balance back and disappeared out of sight, and I thought that was a lot like life.

CHAPTER 10

The notary thing

Life took hold over the next few days, as lesson gave way to lesson which in turn gave way to a few precious minutes where I tried to cobble something together for dinner. The children were back and were making their presence felt. With Anna away at university, the weekly menu had changed overnight from a vegan-friendly feast of grains, pulses and vegetables to the polar opposite in nutritional terms, as the younger siblings celebrated with sausages and burgers the departure of their health-conscious sister. A few delicious days off-duty had made my daily ritual that much harsher. Cosmo was extra-energetic after his stay with Adam who had probably over-exercised him, raising the bar for me on my return. There was too much to do and to think about. My brain struggled to cooperate. I made a mental note to avoid alcohol for a few days, but only a mental one, because I knew myself too well.

Sadie was full of excitement as usual about

the school musical. I rationalised that in the first year of sixth form, she could be allowed a little leeway, and if her grades were suffering slightly, at least she was in a state of joy about something. We all deserved that. It was Wednesday and we were sitting together at the kitchen table, chatting about this and that member of the cast, how many costume changes there were.

"You won't believe how hot it is when I have to wear all the costumes at once in the first scene."

"I can imagine."

The nightclub outfit, then the nun's habit, the work outfit..." She broke off. "You okay Mum?"

"Yes, why?"

"Don't know, just asking."

"I'm fine, just wondering how Josh is getting on."

Her brother was at his third cadet camp that year. It was becoming an obsession.

"He's fine. It's his favourite thing in the world. What are you worried about?"

"Not worried. Sorry. Just feeling thoughtful." I shook myself out of reverie and back into reality. Sadie needed listening to more than I needed to overthink my life.

"Anyway, so like I was saying, I have to wear this fur coat on top of the whole work outfit...."

The rang. I glanced down at it then apologetically back at Sadie, who scraped her chair back and clunked her plate noisily into the sink. I stepped outside, sank into the seat on the terrace and listened to his voice.

"You okay babe?"

"All the better for hearing you. How are you?"

"I'm good. All good. I was thinking about Spain, you know I have to go and do the notary thing."

With all the goings on I had forgotten about that. He had to sign over his apartment in Javea to avoid Spanish inheritance tax. Sensible and underhand at the same time, he was a clearly a man of many disguises, but shared his plans with me as if I was on his team, privy to the master strategy.

"Oh yes, I remember."

"So, I was wondering, when are you free to go out there with me?"

My heart soared and fluttered. I jumped up and headed back into the kitchen where I flicked through my diary. The pages were crammed with crossings out, urgent shopping lists, students changing slots, birthday reminders and red circles round the days I was not going to either smoke or drink a drop of wine, the mental notes having been ignored so far.

"How about the first of June?"

He booked the tickets while I was on the phone to him. I was expecting to have to give my passport details, but he just wanted the spelling of my middle name, and to confirm my date of birth. I waited on the line while he completed the booking, business class, British Airways, civilised flight times… His generosity was boundless, it seemed.

His real name, he admitted at some point around then, was Jonathan. His mum called him Jonathan. Harry was a nickname from childhood. *Flash Harry*, I thought. That works. *Dirty Harry*. That didn't sound so good.

He told me about his flat, where we'd go, who I'd meet, what we'd do. It would be hot by then. Cocktails at Sammy's bar in the old town, stargazing from his roof terrace, dinner on a friend's yacht. I was dizzy with excitement.

Sadie had gone upstairs. Alone in the kitchen now, I sat back down and tried to digest it all. Could this really be happening to me? Was he real? Was this it?

My lessons went better than ever that week. I felt on top of the world and at the top of my game, approved of, valued, needed. Someone was making plans for me, for us, buying me a holiday. This was surely love in its most magical form.

I asked Harry to send me the email confirmation and he agreed but seemed to keep forgetting.

I reminded him once, dressing it up as *"so I have something to look forward to"* and got a curt *"what's your problem baby?"* in response, so I decided to leave it, labelling it as an exercise in letting go of control. I ought to trust him. You can't go anywhere in a relationship without trust. He even said it himself. *"Trust me baby"*. As a gesture of defiance against the box-ticker that I was, and in a bid to rid myself of the control freak label, I threw caution to the wind and left him at the helm.

CHAPTER 11

Nicky

Harry called me the next Friday night, just as I was on my way out to a school reunion. I picked up a note of jealousy in his parting words "have fun with your friends".

In the bright lights of the restaurant, glasses clinked and the girls asked about my romantic adventures. Everything sounded plausible when I retold it, so with every new get-together I became more entrenched in the story, telling it as if it was my own, explaining how the Seatseller app worked, why it was such an innovation, how it was going to transform the whole anti-terror struggle.

People want to put you in a relationship box – *So, are you in one or not?* And now that I was in one, that took me off the worry list for a bit, and they didn't need much more detail.

I sent Harry pictures of my food and my friends, to show him, in case he was worried, that I was indeed dining out with a motley crew of female pals. He called me a couple of times during the meal, which surprised me, but I didn't pick up or check voicemail until I got home. With the backlog of messages it took me a while to piece together what had been going on, but it turned out that Neil and Cass had had a row and the police had been called. Harry had brought Neil to his house and gone off to see a friend called Nicky. I'd heard about Nicky. *"My best female friend"* he had said, in the same breath as mentioning she was an ex hooker and heroin addict.

Jealousy knocked on the door of my heart and left, unwelcome, and then, just as I was falling asleep, the phone rang. I pressed answer, but didn't speak, because I realised I was listening to Harry talking to Nicky. The words were brutal, disjointed. I held my breath as the conversation played out.

Him: I'm in love with her

Her: Bollocks, you just think you are.

Him: No, listen to me Nicky. I am in love with her, whether you like it or not.

Her: I don't care what you fucking think You're out of your mind. You're drunk.

Him: I'm not drunk.

Her: She sounds like a loser

Him: You think so, yeah? You're saying the girl I love is a loser?

Her: She sounds like a fucking loser to me.

Him: Nic.... Look

Her: What?

There was the clink of bottle against glass before she spoke again

Her: You've drunk all my fucking booze.

Him: Nic, she's on the phone

Her: She's what?

Him: She's on the phone. Do you want to talk to her?

There was a silence, and I imagined her horrified face, a mix of incomprehension and humiliation as he handed her the phone. There was a whispered "What the fuck?" and then she was there, bright and clear, and I still hadn't spoken a word. On the phone to me, Nicky's voice went from cockney to Roedean, from rude to charming, from drunk and slurred to the measured sobriety of a kale smoothie sipping yoga teacher, and I thought to myself – what a skill to have. She has the chameleon act down to a t.

I don't know what we spoke about. The only message that got through to me was that this was a man who would stand up for me, for us, and would throw to the lions anyone who dared stand in our way.

I didn't dwell on why he stayed that night at Nicky's house on the sofa, why he didn't get an Uber home, having got one to go there. In my world, I was learning to trust, to live without detailed explanations and to accept shades of grey.

CHAPTER 12

Smitten

We spent the following evening at my house, with Jess and her boyfriend Jason. Harry and I shared with them the unique achievement of having defied all odds by meeting The One on Tinder and Jess and I beamed with mutual smugness as the boys got on like a house on fire. We stepped outside for a cigarette and I asked her what she thought of my Harry, who was standing at the cooker frying up some chillies and garlic. It really was the picture of domestic bliss.

“He says he loves me.” I said.

“That’s okay. That’s good, isn't it?”

“I’m just not sure I feel that way. I don’t know if I can.”

She took a drag of her cigarette and paused for a moment as she observed him adding chopped onions to the pan.

“You can let yourself love him.”

I let the words sink in, imagining I would

feel instantly flooded with emotion, but there was nothing. I wondered if I had been disappointed so many times that now there was a stone where my heart should be.

"I still don't know, Jess. I'm a bit on edge."

"There's such a flow between you two," she observed. "He has such clean energy, such a good heart."

Harry dished up a concoction without a name that tasted delicious, but after a bit of alcohol most things do. We chatted till after midnight, Harry talking about the app he was developing and the deadlines that were coming up. He seemed to tense visibly as Jason asked about some of the detail.

"Tell me more about the app. How does it work on the technical front?" Then, "What kind of ongoing support do you need? Sounds pretty expensive to run, or is it free with the season ticket and the club takes the hit? I mean that makes sense, seeing as they benefit too."

Harry poured himself another drink. "The thing is, we're still testing what we've got, and everything will depend on the meeting with the FA. What they decide could send the whole development in one of many directions."

"I'd love to see the design. I've worked on a few apps like this before."

"Ah, you just want to steal my secrets,"

joked Harry, slapping Jason on the shoulder with a convivial guffaw. "Well I'll show you when it's all in the bag. Until then… " He patted the side of his nose and poured more wine into Jason's glass.

"Cheers." We clinked glasses.

It was nearly one when they left. Jess gave Harry a long hug that seemed to disconcert him slightly. "I'm not used to hugs" he said afterwards, and I thought about his broken home childhood and wanted to fix everything for him. In bed that night, I held him tight, protecting him from the big bad world outside. He wanted sex. I let him make love to me but my head was elsewhere, trying to figure it all out, making no sense of anything.

While I was working the next day, he went to meet Jason at Jess' café – a new venture she had named *Ruby's*, after her most treasured rose quartz bracelet that Jason had given her, He and Jess were moving to Surrey soon, and Harry had generously offered his house as a jumping off point for viewings if they wanted to stay there for a weekend before he moved out. Sharing is caring, and we were all like some kind of extended happy family. He came back full of beans, or full of something, because he should have been much more hungover.

"I like Jason. He's a good bloke."

"I'm glad. They're good friends of mine."

Harry loved my friends as much as they

loved him, and when he started hanging around a bit more, it seemed like the most natural thing in the world. I'm still not sure how that happened, when it started, and what the agreement was, but he was just there a lot, his underwear was in the washing basket and there were a couple of shirts hanging in the cupboard. Maya came by one evening on her way home from Waitrose, free coffee and newspaper in hand, and gave him the once over. He teased her for walking a mile for news that was a day old and caffeine that would keep her up all night. She teased him back for doing the washing up *"I see Rach has got you where she wants you..."* and I relaxed. He fitted into my life like water.

My children seemed to accept the new arrival in our home without protest, but then protesting wasn't their style. When Josh arrived back from camp to find my new boyfriend in the car with me waiting outside school, he showed no reaction at all, and if he was surprised to find him still in our house two days later, I never knew. I didn't ask how he or Sadie felt about any of it, and I am ashamed to say I didn't even try to explain in any detail, but presented the new relationship as a fait accompli.

It was easy enough for me to do. At fifteen and sixteen, Josh and Sadie spent most of their time holed up in their rooms watching who knew what on Netflix and YouTube, and communicating with the outside world via Instagram and Snapchat. Occasionally they would convene in the kitchen to get each others' views on exactly which filter they should use on a particular photograph, lining up the alternatives which I couldn't tell apart. They worked on this digital showreel with the dedication of Michelangelo painting the Sistine Chapel, and it was impossible to tell if they even noticed my existence, let alone that of a new man in our midst.

Sadie was charming, welcoming, funny, showing a level of maturity beyond her sixteen years. During the later years of my marriage to Adam, and throughout the five years since our separation, she had learnt to present a public face which betrayed none of the pain underneath, and that was what she showed to Harry, for as long as she could.

It was Maddie who pointed it out, when Harry was at work, or somewhere. I never knew exactly where he went, and I didn't always ask, because he would frown and want to know why I wanted to know. Maddie called to see how things were. I said everything was wonderful. I told her about our upcoming trip to Spain, about Harry renting the Dorset house again for me in August, how I was the luckiest woman alive. Then she asked about the children.

"Have you asked them what they think of him?"

"Not exactly."

"Do you think you should say something, I mean, just see where they are with it?"

"I should, I suppose."

"I think it would be good if you could have the conversation, just to let them know you're still there, you still care, you know."

"They know I love them." I felt myself tense up, the way you do if you feel someone question your fundamental role in life.

"Not necessarily. Not always. Children need reassurance. They don't like change. They can see new arrivals as a threat."

"I feel bad now. It kind of feels too late."

"How too late?"

"I don't know – it just feels like he's already got his feet under the table."

We let those words hang in the air between us. I brushed away a flicker of uncertainty.

The next day, as if by some strange kink of fate, Harry announced that he might not be able to see me for a few days. He needed to go to the office, not just to pick up his Mercedes that was languishing in the underground car park, but to make things happen, get his team to realise that apps don't build themselves, that there was a deadline to meet, and that the new football season was only a few months away. He'd be letting them know in no uncertain terms that if Seatseller wasn't in place then, and on the smartphones of all season ticket holders in the country, there would be hell to pay. I imagined that being on the receiving end of Harry's wrath would be an ordeal you wouldn't want to repeat. There was a fierce look in his eye I hadn't seen before. I wanted to temper it. I tried suggesting he take a more diplomatic approach, but he turned to me with disbelief verging on fury.

"These guys need kicking. I can't afford to get this wrong. You don't understand what happens if we are *one day late.*"

"I do understand," I ventured, "but I just think you need to focus on getting the best out of them, don't you?"

"You don't want to see me when I get mad babe. And you gotta trust me, remember? I know what I'm doing." His last few words slowed to a crawl, as if I was too stupid to understand.

The week that followed brought back a sense of normality and belonging I hadn't realised was missing in my tiny family. We played cards, watched TV together and I laughed at YouTube videos of dogs and cats not getting along. I ferried Sadie to and from rehearsals, Josh to swimming club, and we ate sausages and burgers for dinner. I tidied their rooms, filled the dishwasher three times a day and somehow managed to teach a few students in between.

An evening with Maddie, Maya and Jess

brought home to me just how much things had changed, and how quickly. We walked up the hill to the pub and sat outside under the heaters, as various acquaintances passed by, said hello, asked after the children, told me about theirs. That night was an oasis, a stopping point where everything could have changed, a fork in the road, a chance to escape, which I didn't take.

"Chris texted me today." Maddie announced, out of the blue.

"Not again!" Maya was half laughing, half sighing. "Why does everyone else have men texting them all the time while I'm stuck with one that doesn't even look at me?"

"You don't have to be stuck with him" Jess pointed out. "Don't forget I was once where you are, and now Jason and I, we're..." she tailed off, biting her lip suddenly.

"You're what?"

"I shouldn't be telling you. I mean, we haven't told the kids."

"We promise not to tell your kids," I said, prodding her, "go on..."

"I think we know what she's not saying, don't we?" Maddie grinned around the table, herding us together with her bright smile that may have hidden a thousand tears. I wouldn't have thought that if Maya hadn't mentioned it, but now she seemed suddenly vulnerable.

"I think, congratulations...." I raised my glass.

"Thank you," said Jess, suddenly more coy teenager than a forty something divorcee.

"I'm happy for you," I said. When I said it, it sounded odd. I mean, why wouldn't I be happy for her? But I'm not always happy for couples if I'm truly honest. I have clicked Like on their Facebook posts and their anniversary photos with clichéd Hallmark captions. But they are raising the bar, challenging me to be as blissed out as they are, and I panic because I'm never going to manage it. Then there are the couples I don't even know, holding hands in the street, kissing at the station, wandering into cafés on a Sunday morning, tousled and hungry after a night of passionate love-making. I make up stories about Cassandra who inhabits a world I don't belong in and will never be part of.

Thankfully, some of the less lucky ones find themselves alone again on the outside with me. We say we are safe here, but we are all secretly dreaming of having another chance.

Maddie was full of questions for Jess, not just about when and where this wedding would be, but more importantly, how were all the children, from both sides of the relationship, going to feel about it, did his ex know yet, and how was she likely to take the news. Maddie was always thinking about the feelings of those who weren't in the frame. If she was looking at a photograph of a group of happy couples, she'd be wondering if the photographer felt left out. But Jess met all her concerns with calm reassurance, and we were satisfied that on this occasion, a much-maligned dating app had against all odds delivered a true-life romance with a happy ending.

"So, Maya, like I said," Jess put her hand on Maya's arm and stroked it as she spoke, which Maya would have found incredibly awkward, but didn't let on. "You don't have to be with Simon forever. Your life isn't over yet. You're gorgeous and intelligent and you need to be with someone who appreciates you for everything that you are."

Maya and I exchanged glances. We had been through this so many times, but it was always worth another shot. Maya listed the reasons she couldn't leave – her reasons, not watertight but hers nonetheless. I turned to Jess.

"I just think things have to reach rock bottom for those two. They haven't yet. It's still bearable, and Maya would feel too guilty."

"And more to the point, she can see the mess we make of our lives and probably thinks she's better off staying with him," Maddie added. That was true enough. Maddie's personal life was enough to make anyone take shelter in a convent and take a vow of silence.

"So who is this Chris? Remind me," asked Maya again, shaking her gin and tonic to bring us to attention with the jangle of ice bells. "I mean, I know you're head over heels in love, but what's his story?"

Maddie's face erupted in a grin.

"A friend of Rachel's from college, and I'm totally and utterly smitten." She spoke the last words slowly and with emphasis, drawing us in with her absolutes.

"Ooh, I'd like to be smitten," said Maya. "Remind me how it feels?"

"We met at a party. We couldn't take our eyes off each other. I think he feels the same, in fact I know he does. It was one of those moments..."

"And he's married," I added.

"Yes, that's the problem," admitted Maddie, almost downcast for a split second.

"Tricky. I see." Maya and I exchanged glances.

"It doesn't have to be a problem, of course." I had a feeling Jess would say that. She saw opportunities in everything, in everyone. She believed in relationships as training grounds for self-development, and would never rule something out on grounds of boundaries put in place many years ago by naïve lovers.

"He's been with her what? Twenty-five years? They might have grown apart in that time. They might not be right for each other anymore. Who knows? She might be unhappy with him and want him to leave."

"Absolutely" agreed Maya. "I wish Simon would take the hint and do that."

Jess gave her a look and she laughed. "Okay, I know. I take it back."

We let Maddie wax lyrical about love for a while. Then my phone beeped and I took the opportunity to glance at the message under the table. It was an answer to my text from earlier, asking how he was getting on with the whip-cracking.

What do you mean, babe? I'm at work here. It's going to be a long night.

I hesitated before replying. Placate, placate.

I'm sure you're doing a great job. Thinking of you xx

Where are you?

I hesitated again before texting back that I was at home, in bed. Then I was on my feet, in a hurry to leave, make it all true, keep him happy. I left the girls at the bar ordering one for the road muttered an excuse about the kids and slipped away.

Something was wrong, but I put it down to my insecurity, to my being unused to this. I didn't know how to behave, how far to be me, how far to be what he wanted me to be. But then I didn't really know what that was either.

All I did know was that actually being apart

from Harry was torture. I was forever wondering where he was, who with, what he was doing. He was stressed when we spoke on the phone the next day, didn't seem to want to give me the answers I wanted, just supplied information I didn't really need. There had been a crisis at work, a malfunction in the coding which had led to his father, the rags to riches super-engineer, having to fly over from Spain to take the reins. Harry was reluctant to go cap in hand to the man who had failed so dismally as a father, but they agreed on a percentage shareholding that he would receive for responding to the SOS and throwing his team of experts into the mix. The deadline for delivering his final presentation to the FA was only days away and an issue like this could sent the whole project spiralling into disaster.

From his messages alone, the tension was palpable and contrasted so sharply with our happy times that I felt lost, grappling for reassurance in a vacuum that offered nothing more than curt put-downs. Harry was tired and grumpy and not his usual self when we next spoke. By now we hadn't seen each other for four days and nights and I couldn't sleep. I'd look at when he was last online, fret about why he was up so late. Finally, he rang, and I answered practically before the first ring. It was 10.25 am.

"I tried calling you last night,"I said.

"I know baby, I was out with my Dad and

Neil"

Neil was by all accounts his father's lapdog and IT fix-all.

"Where did you go?"

"Out for dinner"

"Was it okay?"

"Not really, no. Nothing's okay right now babe. You've just got to bear with me."

"Things will work out. You were up late." Trying to calm him never worked. I don't know why I thought it would.

"What do you mean?"

"WhatsApp – last seen 3.30 am"

"I've told you about that babe. What's going on with you?"

"Nothing. Sorry, I was just worried about you."

"Look, it might be a few more days until we can see each other, with all this stuff going on. I can't tell you how long, but you need to bear with me."

"You said that already."

There was the familiar sound of a ring pull, the pop and fizz of a can being opened.

"Thirsty?"

"Jack Daniels and coke."

"Harry, it's half past ten in the morning."

"Is it?" Then in a more muffled tone I heard "Oi mate, you got a light?"

Harry didn't smoke. I let it go. This wasn't a normal situation, so normal behaviour couldn't be expected.

The phone rang again a few minutes later, before I'd had time to gather my thoughts. The ringtone put a smile on my face and banished the tension from my shoulders because it was my Charlie Dimmock friend and soulmate.

"Sal, what a lovely surprise. How are things?"

"Fine, well, not entirely, if I'm honest."

"Go on."

"Have you got a minute?"

"I've got plenty of minutes. Next student isn't till this afternoon. Knock yourself out."

Sally hesitated. "Okay so I did what you suggested."

"What did I suggest? Sorry, I can't even remember." I thought back to our last conversation. It seemed like an age ago.

"About asking Sylvia, the woman who lives at the end of the road in the big house, you know, to be my spy."

"Oh, okay, that was brave. What happened?"

"She did it. She was delighted to do it in fact. Said lots of stuff about women sticking together, swore herself to secrecy without even being asked. It was great, just having that conversation, feeling supported."

"I'm sensing a but."

"Yes, there is a but. It sounds a bit worrying."

"Worrying how? God I feel bad now for suggesting it. I didn't actually think anything would come of it, just reassurance for you I guess, and for me."

"Obviously she couldn't hear the other side of the conversation, couldn't even hear Graham clearly, but it was more the body language. She said he was pacing up and down, hands through his hair, seemed really stressed. Raised his voice saying something like 'I know. I'm doing my best. It won't be for long.' And hung up the phone without saying goodbye, then rang back to apologise, said he missed her, thought about her all the time."

"What are you thinking? I mean, it could be his daughter, she's 14, might have been giving him some grief?"

"That's possible, I suppose it could have been Chloe, although it seems a bit tempestuous and romantic for a father daughter chat. It's just, when he came back, and this was obviously before I heard back from Sylvia, he was all jolly and saying how he'd had a lovely chat with Jack about his school project."

"No mention of Chloe?"

"No mention."

"Maybe don't read too much into this. It is hearsay, after all." I was deeply regretting my suggestion of involving a third party, but it was too late now.

"There is one other thing."

"Go on."

"Apparently the ex has bought tickets for the Lion King. Happy families and all that."

"Look Sally, I know it's hard, but what choice do you have but to go along with it? I mean, unless you want a big screaming row, which I can't imagine leading anywhere. If you want to be with him, well, this is him, and you have to either trust him or have it out with him and let things take their course." I felt I wasn't making any sense.

"I tried to broach the subject, but he was vile to me. Told me it was none of my business, that his life was complicated enough. Then the next day he said he'd seen his sister-in-law in town."

"So..."

"Exactly. I asked him if he'd said hello and he asked me if I was some kind of idiot. How could I not realise that was a problem for him."

"He didn't want word to get back to her?"

"I assume so, and he is now saying he'll never go back there because it's too risky."

"Who does he think he is? Lord Lucan?"

"And he won't hold my hand in the street anymore. Told me off the next day when I tried to. Said no more PDAs. I felt so ashamed."

"How dare he treat you like that?" It was a rhetorical question, to which I knew the answer. People only treat us badly if we allow them to, and if there was one lesson I had learnt from the Archers, as well as my own life, to a lesser extent, it was that abuse can take many forms besides physical violence.

"Then the next minute he's all sorry and loving and making me laugh. It's so weird. I feel so miserable. One minute I think he's got to go, and the next, he seems back to his old self and things are better again. But I am feeling so down. I feel unworthy, ugly, not good enough, and then just when I want to give up hope, everything changes and there's a light at the end of the tunnel."

"Then the light goes out, right?"

"It's all about whether or not you make the grade, and more often than not, you don't."

"Just like that."

"They call it gas-lighting. It's a powerful tool, hard to prove, no bruises."

"Oh God, how did we get here Rach?"

I noticed the *we* and felt instantly guarded, because where she was and where I was were clearly, in my view, completely different places.

Harry would never try and control me like Graham did. He was completely open about his past, and certainly wasn't hankering after an ex who wasn't an ex. Things couldn't have been more opposite.

"I don't know, Sally, but I think it sounds like you need to get rid of him."

"I know."

This was the first time she had let that idea stay on the table, and we spent a minute or two sitting with it, in our different houses, sitting on our different sofas, and I remembered the opening line of Anna Karenina – something about all happy families being alike and all unhappy families being unhappy in different ways.

CHAPTER 13

Whatever people say I am, that's what I'm not

Harry and I got through our week apart, talking late into the night and sending each other YouTube videos of songs that spoke about us, or at least I did. Macy Gray *The time of my life,* Carly Simon *Nobody does it better.* He sent me *Would I lie to you* and a song by Arctic Monkeys called *Fake Tales of San Francisco.* I know now that the album it's from is called *Whatever people say I am, that's what I'm not.* On the Wednesday, he Facetimed me again from his house that would soon be in the hands of strangers. It was the family home he'd brought up his children in and it was time to move on. It was too grown up for him, I could see that. And I was excited that he was going to be nearer me.

On the Friday, he said he couldn't wait any longer and was coming to see me. Work could wait. The lackeys could handle it on their own for a day.

I'll be at New Malden station in half an hour.

See you there.

I raced back from walking Cosmo and jumped in the shower, pulling up at the station in my car just in time to see his train arrive. He climbed into the passenger seat, and after the usual *"You okay baby?"* told me what had happened to him on the way. He spoke without drama or emotion, looking straight ahead, strangely unfazed, with the occasional glance in my direction. With my eyes on the road, I didn't think anything of it, but I know I wouldn't have been that calm if it had happened to me. At Godalming station, he had just put his laptop bag down on the bench, when someone asked him if it was the right platform for Guildford. As he spoke to one of the men, his laptop was snatched by the other. He didn't actually realise he'd been robbed until he was getting on the train, whereupon the scam fell into place. He said he felt stupid, but he had things on his mind and lost all concentration.

"That's awful. What are you going to do? Did you report it?"

"Yes they're looking at the CCTV already I think. Apparently, it's happened before and they think they know who the little fuckers are. It's such a classic MO."

"It's easily done. Such a shame we can't trust people."

"They won't be able to get into it either. And it's traceable, so they'll need to get rid of it quick."

"I'm sorry. Horrible start to the day."

"I was going to show you the app, baby."

"How are you going to manage? How are you going to do your meeting next week without the laptop?"

"Oh, it's all on the cloud and it's all insured. My cards get replaced within 24 hours. There was only about £150 in cash in there."

Only? I would have been in bits if I'd lost that much.

I thought *this man is strong and brave and rich and not attached to material things*. I forgot about the Mercedes, the Ducati, the Kawasaki and the Rolex watch.

"Actually, there is something." He had just come off the phone with his Dad. They seemed to be talking all the time now, cooking up plans to rescue the ticketing app in time for the following week.

"Anything."

"If you could get me a few hundred quid out of the bank, my Dad can make a transfer to you online."

The logic of this suggestion failed to compute.

"Why him? Can't *you* do a transfer to me online?"

I don't think he answered my question, but nothing more was said about providing a bridging loan, so I let it go.

We spent the day in Putney looking at properties for him to spend a proportion of his substantial rental income on – concierge-serviced apartments overlooking the Thames with gyms, pools and underground car parks. From time to time, there were phone calls to and from the police, giving more details, getting crime reference numbers and updates on the search for the scoundrels in question. I paid for lunch at Carluccio's – salads and Sauvignon Blanc in the sunshine, while in the back of my mind I pictured where we'd be in a few weeks' time, in the beach bars of the Costa Blanca, sipping sangria in the sunset at restaurants he described in detail that only a regular would remember. What goes around comes around, and I would have my turn.

Harry was the very epitome of charm with the estate agents, making each one feel like their property had that special something he was looking for. Effusive in gratitude, he left them smiling and hopeful. He pointed out the flat where he was going to be staying in the interim - a kind of accommodation bridge. Mark Rathbone, godfather to his son and a business colleague of his father's, had a spare room. We talked about what it would be like when he was living just a few minutes from me, how we could go out to a riverside bar, meet for breakfast at the Putney canteen. I could even do my lessons in his new flat. He wanted me to move in with him.

Harry, Harry what were you thinking…?

And from there I think it began to fall apart.

CHAPTER 14

Packers

Everyone with a teenage daughter knows where they were the morning after the Manchester bombing. I was in my bedroom throwing clothes into my cupboard, unable to process the news, when the phone rang. I flopped onto the bed to answer it.

"You alright baby?" It was his usual opener, but he seemed genuinely concerned this time.

"Well, I'm a bit shocked. Aren't you?"

"Why what's up?"

"The news."

"Oh that. Well I'm not, to be honest."

"What do you mean?" My heart missed a beat, even before he explained.

"I mean, it was always going to happen. And it makes my product that much more valuable."

I stopped in my tracks. I am ashamed that I didn't just hang up on the spot, finish it, walk away, but I just said: "I can't believe you said that." There was a pause before he replied, and he seemed almost as astounded at my disbelief as I was at his lack of concern.

"Oh, come on baby, you know me. I don't mean it like that. But I 'm always looking for the angle, you know I am."

"Imagine if your child had been there. Imagine for a second how you would feel if one of your children was killed."

And then there was another silence that just made me think I'd made my point.

I drove Sadie to school. It is only a twenty-minute walk, but driving is an opportunity to be together, to talk facing forwards, without the confrontation that eye contact can imply to a self-conscious teenager. I listened to her talk about terrorism, how incomprehensible it was to her that someone could want to kill children. She doesn't cry easily, but tears were filling her eyes as well as mine as she spoke.

It was a sickening coincidence that Harry had his meeting with the FA that day, at which he would demonstrate the workings of the Seatseller app, along with the underlying message that football stadiums around the country would be safe from terrorist attacks if the Association endorsed and enforced this state of the art technology. It wasn't far from blackmail, and he wasn't afraid of admitting it.

I called him back because I hated how we

had left things teetering on a precipice. I wanted to coax him down, placate him, show him that I was there for him.

Meanwhile the removal company was coming to empty his house ahead of the new family moving in. When he answered my call after several rings, I couldn't hear anything in the background. I wondered if he was outside, or in the bathroom, but then there would be the sound of traffic, or an echo. I hesitated for a second before I said anything, in case I provoked a bad reaction.

"It's very quiet."

"What do you mean?"

"The packers are quiet. Are they just wrapping cotton wool in feathers or something?"

"They're upstairs. I'm in my office."

"How does it feel?"

"How does what feel?"

"Getting all your stuff packed up in boxes, giving your home away?"

"It feels good! I'm going to get four and a half grand a month for it. That's good, huh?"

"But don't you feel sad? I would."

"What are you saying baby?"

I stuttered some weak reply, but I must have given away that I just thought something wasn't right. Someone or something had taken the blindfold off and I was dazzled. When he was at my side, in my house, kissing me, loving me, making me tea, trimming the hedge, stacking the dishwasher, I questioned nothing, but on the phone, with the pauses and the questions and his strange reactions to things, I was walking on eggshells. His voice was slurred. Alarm bells rang in my head but I pushed them aside and soldiered on with blind trust.

The journey from New Malden to Godalming takes about forty minutes. There was no traffic and I would be there in good time, although I hadn't asked him what time he was leaving for the meeting. I could have told him I was coming, but I didn't. I could have stayed at home, but I didn't. Our awkward phone calls were plaguing me. Now, only a face-to-face chat would do.

I told myself I was going down there because I wanted to see for myself what was happening, wanted to see him there, in the house he said he was in, the real-life version of the picture he had painted.

But I went there without telling him I was going, because at some level I didn't trust him anymore.

It was a long and hard forty minutes. With every second that went by I wondered what I would find, and the thought of what he might do or say if he knew I was coming kept my heart in my mouth for the whole journey. Adrenaline pumped around my body, surging in my stomach like a tidal wave with nowhere to go. I felt sick, my head pounded, and voice in my head said *turn back*. Pulling off the A3, I almost headed home, out of the firing line and back to where I was expected to be, but the need for answers was too great. I did two loops of the roundabout and followed signs to the station. He lived near the station.

I knew the name of his road but had forgotten the number, despite trying to memorise it when he took me on a Facetime tour of it during one of our early phone calls. I think at the time I was too busy scanning the rooms for evidence of a woman, because that's how these things always end in books isn't it – he turns out to be married...

"Can I come and see you?" I texted him. *"I'm in Godalming."*

"But baby I'm not there anymore. I'm in London."

The phone rang. It was him, his voice edgy, anxious.

"I'm in London babe. What's going on?"

"Where in London? I thought you were at home. You were there less than an hour ago."

"What's this about? I'm at Yo Sushi at Waterloo station. What's going on with you?"

My voice shook as I stuttered a reply. "I didn't think that conversation went very well this morning... I hate it when we have those chats. I wanted to see you... I just drove here to see you, talk to you, make sure we're okay."

He seemed shocked, then calm, as I persuaded him I was in need of his reassurance, that I had only come on a mission of love, and the conversation veered towards things I could do – he offered to meet me in London, told me to get dressed up and come to the FA with him, but the timings were clearly too tight for that. I asked him what number his house was, and with some hesitation he told me. Then he asked:

"Are you actually going round to my house?"

By then I was actually *at* the house, pulling into the drive. In front of the door there was a silver Peugeot that had featured on his video. He had bought it for his son and it was decommissioned, awaiting some repairs. That made sense. I got out of the car and walked over to the Peugeot. On the back seat was a cushion embroidered with the word LOVE, and on the passenger seat a USB cable lay in a tangle. I peered through the stained-glass window by the front door. On the windowsill sat a row of glass and china ornaments that seemed unlikely possessions for a single man. The hall was full of normal furniture for a hall, an umbrella holder, a coat stand, a small table, and on the bottom stair, a pile of clothes, a blue shirt, a pair of shiny black shoes. A door was ajar leading to a room to the right of the hall. My heart raced with inexplicable excitement mixed with fear. This was his home, where I had expected to find him, surrounded by packing boxes, pacing the floor, practising his presentation to the FA. Yet what I found was a fully furnished house with a car in the drive and not a van or removal man in sight. He was still on the line.

“There are no packers here Harry.”

“They must have left.”

“The house is still full of stuff.”

“They were doing the upstairs today. They’re coming back to do the rest tomorrow. What is this?”

My heart was pounding, but I carried on, riding some sort of wave of bravery, with no regard for the riptide that might drag me under at any moment. I was staring at the gap between the door to the sitting room and the door frame. I could just make out a television screen, flashing with images of what must have been a house decoration programme.

“The door to the lounge is open. There’s someone in there watching TV”

“What do you mean?”

“What do you think I mean?” I regretted the words as they were said. There was a pause full of his anger. I rang the doorbell. No action in the TV room. Either someone had been warned to stay put, or that someone was him.

“So, I must have left the TV on. What’s going

on Rachel? Are you going to go through the bins now?"

"Good idea." Either he was watching me, in which case I couldn't dig myself in any deeper, or he wasn't, and he would never know. I lifted the lids and found the usual black bin bags, the normal recycling – papers and bottles. Was that usual though? Daily Telegraph and Bordeaux – could be anyone, or could it? I was perplexed.

"Go round the back, why don't you. Take a look at the view." He was goading me now, like the guy in the movie saying *"Go on then, shoot me"*.

I did as he asked, maybe because I thought he was watching, the terrorist in a Hollywood thriller controlling everything you do or he'll detonate the bomb. Now I realise that I was providing whoever was in the lounge with the necessary time to escape.

The back garden was just as he had shown me on Facetime, lawn perfectly manicured, stunning views over the Surrey hills. A cuckoo called invisibly from the laurel hedge. Cuckoos are a bizarre birds. How could it be worth all that hassle dumping your eggs with other birds just for a bit of free babysitting? I still wonder how a whole species can display psychopathic behaviour as the basis for their own survival and get away with it, whereas in the human race it would be seen as an anomaly, a malfunction, or at least something to be swept under the carpet.

Harry was silent but still on the line. I hung up.

Just inside the back door I could see a pair of flip flops. They were black, which to me, on some sexist level, suggested a man, but they were smaller than I thought they would be. I moved closer to the window, my hand forming a bridge between my forehead and the glass to keep out the sun's reflection. On the kitchen surfaces were the usual bits and pieces, a jar of instant coffee, a sugar bowl, a used mug by the sink. On the fridge, I could see what looked like invitations, photographs, business cards, all the usual paraphernalia stuck by magnets to its shiny front. On a table at the far end was a photograph in a frame of two figures I couldn't identify, and next to that another one of a baby, a big close up of a grinning face and floppy blonde locks. That must be his son, I thought, but I wanted to see his face, to see Harry's face in this little boy, to be reminded that the baby had a daddy, and that there was a bond between them that nobody had a right to break.

I tried taking a photo with my phone on zoom and then zooming in on the result, but the picture was blurred. Then, without thinking, I found myself trying the door, which opened easily, and before I knew it, I was inside, standing on soft beige carpet, taking in my surroundings. There was a smell of bacon. I was about to take a step towards the hallway, but a tiny sound from above made me stop in my tracks. I stood rooted to the spot. Overhead there was the scrape of furniture on the floor and then silence.

I waited what must have been a minute or two without moving, except to reach slowly into my pocket and silence my phone. The back door creaked open and I held it still, my hand shaking, before stepping outside again and shutting it carefully. I made my way back to the front of the house as quietly as possible and headed to my car. I thanked God and the universe for not letting the phone ring while I was in there.

It was time to go home. I drove away, but stopped a few yards down the road, watching the house because some time, someone would need to come out of there.

At that moment, like a prisoner on the run in the precious minutes when the searchlights fall elsewhere, I went into full investigation mode. For a milisecond, the scales had been lifted from my eyes and I was alive to reality. I looked up the registration of the silver Peugeot on a vehicle ownership records site, but couldn't find a name, only the date of purchase and the fact that the brakes needed fixing. I looked up the house on the land registry and found it to be in the name of Mr Daniel and Mrs Joanne Stone. I looked up Seat-seller again online, this time on the Companies House register and found that this was indeed the current registered address, but it had previously been listed as an address in Sunningdale. The company had been set up in February with two £1 shares and two shareholders: Mr Harry Dawson and Miss Samantha Brize. So this would be Sam, the *bloke* he'd set up the business with.

With my pulse still racing and adrenaline flooding my system, I had to think fast. He had told me the meeting was scheduled for 2pm. I googled the phone number of the FA and asked to speak to the secretary to the board of directors. I was surprised to be put through at all, but within a second, a bored sounding woman answered the phone and I scrambled for words, settling in the end for directness.

"Do you happen to know if a Mr Harry Dawson is having a meeting with the board this afternoon?"

There was a pause.

"Nothing here in the diary." Another pause. "But then I wouldn't be able to divulge that information."

She already had, as far as I was concerned.

I called Grants' Estate Agents, and they confirmed they had had nothing for sale in that road for the last six months at least.

The roller coaster had reached its peak and was in free fall; the ground had been pulled from under me. I drove to Ruby's café where I smoked three cigarettes in succession, telling Jess everything. She has always been a bit of a philosopher, a stoic optimist and believer in relationships as the healing environment for childhood wounds. *"We can't learn to trust in theory, we need to practise it."* Was her mantra. Together we had lived through romantic successes and failures, mostly failures, but she and Jason were solid now, and she attributed that to the ethos she upheld having paid off over time. She hadn't run away when things got difficult. And here I was about to do exactly that, so she was going to set me right again.

"I'm talking to him on the phone and he's at home watching the house getting packed up, then when I turn up at his house forty-five minutes later, he's apparently at Waterloo Station."

"He could have easily got to London in that time."

"But what about the packers? They weren't even there. The house was full of stuff."

"Maybe they had gone, maybe they had cleared the upstairs like he said."

"Where was his motorbike, his car?"

"I don't know. At the garage? Like he said they were? Didn't he say the other night that the bike needed the seat adjusting and his friend was doing it?" She remembered more than I did. Perhaps I was losing my mind. I fought that thought.

"I heard a noise. There was someone upstairs."

"You think you did – it could have been your imagination. Sometimes we hear things we expect to hear, almost to confirm our own fears." I felt small, mistaken, deluded.

"And the house has never even been on the market. I called the agents," I said weakly, tears rising behind my eyes again.

"It may have been a different branch, and didn't you say it was off the books or something?"

I inhaled deeply on my cigarette before stubbing it out in the ashtray. She was still looking at me with the kindest, most loving gaze any human being could bestow. Her heart was holding hands with mine. I wanted to believe her, almost felt I'd let her down if I didn't. My faith in Jess was unquestioning. Trained in psychology, NLP and no doubt all sorts of other things, she had a view on life that was enviable. Everything that happened was meant to teach us something and I had to endure, experience, absorb what was happening in order to learn my lesson, whatever it might be. But I was resisting now. I had a feeling this was a lesson I might have already learnt, and that now was the time to recognise that and step away.

"I'm scared Jess. Something's not right. I know you said we had a good connection and I thought we did too. We get on so well, we laugh, it's beautiful, but he's lying to me and I don't know why. He says he isn't, but he is, I know he is, and now you make it sound like he's not and I think

I'm going mad."

Jess nodded with all the earnestness of someone who really truly believes you. When someone believes you, you believe them back. That's just what happened then.

"Honey, this is all part of the journey. You aren't running away, you're staying and finding out, you're trusting instead of escaping. You are amazing, Rachel. Stay with this and you will experience so much growth, so much development. Harry is teaching you something, and you are teaching him something. Relationships are where the learning happens, remember."

I did remember. She calmed my hysteria, and my tears dried on my face. I went home and tidied the house in the frantic way you do when you feel things are out of control. Harry texted something at 1.55 and I thought – *why aren't you practising your presentation to the board?* Then he texted again at 3.30, no mention of how the meeting went. I asked. He just said *fine*.

I had just finished teaching when the phone went. He was outside the Wetherspoons in New Malden. He had a surprise for me.

"I just need to see you baby. I don't like it when we fight."

"I will be there. Give me five minutes."

I'm not sure where the doubts went, the anger, the fear, the hysteria, but one look at his blue eyes and big smile and I was all his, *one hundred and fifty percent*, as they say on *Love Island*. I just had one condition.

"I just need to tell you something first." I had hardly sat down, but I needed to get it out before I had a drink and changed my mind.

"What's that, baby?"

"You can't stay at my house tonight." There. It was out. I had taken some sort of control back. Or so I thought.

"Ok!" He put up his hands in defence. "I wasn't expecting anything, just wanted to see you. What's up with you? You look shaken up."

"I am a bit, after this morning."

"But why? I thought I explained it all to you."

"It was just a shock. I thought I'd find you there, with all the boxes, and there was no you and no boxes. Makes me worried you're lying to me about something. Did the packers really come?"

"Baby, it's all fine. It's all true. If you went down there first thing tomorrow morning you'd find the packers there. Honest."

"Okay." I took a sip of my wine. He had bought a bottle but I could barely manage a glass. I got up to leave. Sadie would be back home from rehearsals any minute and I wanted to be there. He caught my hand, looked into my eyes.

"I love you."

"I know."

"And I know." He meant he knew I loved him too. I didn't put him right, but I never said it back.

"Are we good, baby?"

"We're good." But I had noticed the shirt he was wearing. It was the one I'd seen that morning on the stairs of his house, and now I knew who had been watching TV with the door ajar.

CHAPTER 15

Pitfalls

Relationships are full of pitfalls, but the best bit is getting through the bad times, laughing at yesterday's issues, repackaging them in today's newly acquired self-knowledge. I haven't necessarily mastered the art of laughing at myself but it's on the list.

But humour is a subjective thing. What amuses me doesn't necessarily amuse others, especially if they, like me, haven't perfected the art of being taken for a ride. Texting humour is even trickier. Love affairs have ended over an e-mail written too casually being taken too seriously, and even a strategically placed emoji can be overlooked by an over-sensitive recipient. I regularly found myself on both sides of the fence, but it didn't seem to make me any more careful. Usually, a decent explanation and apology can go a long way to build bridges, but that was not the case here.

I was making tea in the kitchen the next

morning when I noticed Harry's first message of the day.

Morning. How are you?

I hesitated. I imagined him sitting in his house, the house I now presumed to be his parents' house, conscious of the storm we had sailed through the previous day. He was checking in to see where we were, if there was any damage to the hull, and whether repairs were required. My instinct was to show him, with as much humour as I could muster, that the structure of HMS Relationship was intact. But that humour misfired, with horrific consequences.

Marvellous, but I can't see any packers...

His reply was instantaneous.

Are you at my house?

I ignored his question, asking him instead

Where are you???

I read his answer, hearing his voice in my head, and glad it was only words on a screen, without volume or tone.

What is going on Rachel? FFS. My mum's there

I ignored his call which followed immediately, and just texted back:

Only joking

Well I'm not laughing

The minutes that followed were torture. My tea went cold, I made another cup and that went cold too. I looked at our messages over and over again. I was an idiot. Why had I thought that this was a good idea? At no point had he given me any indication that he could laugh at himself. We had never reached the point of looking back at a misunderstanding and taking responsibility. Harry wasn't a forgiving person. Then I thought – *but this is me being me.* I am the person that laughs at the past, that can make a joke out of the trials of yesterday to pave way for new beginnings, and why is that wrong?

I knew the answer to that. It was wrong because it was wrong for him, and anything that was wrong for him would sooner or later be wrong for me.

The phone rang again half an hour later and when I steeled myself to answer I had my first taste of Harry's rage. He made a point of telling me this was the nice version, that he'd calmed himself before calling me and I *didn't want to know* what he was like before. He'd used his *ten minute wait rule* before getting back in touch, and I ought to be grateful for that. He'd had to leave work, he was worried for his mum's well-being because she was sitting in the house waiting for the packers. He had told her to go round to the safety of a neighbour's house, because he was suddenly afraid I was a crazed bunny boiler rampaging through Surrey. Having walked out of the office in fury, he was now heading home to let the packers in himself, fuming, raging. He said I should tell my friends what I had done, to see what they thought of my disgusting behaviour, that I should take a hard look at myself, that he was rethinking how he felt about me, that I had triggered something that wasn't going to just go away and there would be consequences.

I sent a desperately placatory message back, contrite, remorseful.

His replies were unrelenting.

The packers turned up and there was no one here so I have had to pay for their time today and they can't come back till the weekend.

I was back where he wanted me. I just said *I'm sorry*

You've really fucked things up for me you know.

Then an hour later, as I sat huddled in the corner of the sofa staring at my phone, wanting to take it all back, be different, be better, he rang back, said we should put it behind us. He asked if we were good, and I said yes.

On WhatsApp that afternoon he was back to his old self, briefly. We talked about plans for the upcoming weekend. I had been invited to spend a day sailing with Caro and James and there was room for one more. It had been agreed I could bring Harry. The others were curious to meet him. It made sense that I should stay over in Godalming on the Saturday night, so that it would be a shorter journey down to the river Hamble the next morning. Staying at his place was just an idea, brewing, as yet unspoken, and I hadn't worked out where we would sleep if all the rest of the furniture was getting taken away that day by those elusive packers, but my opportunity to suggest it came when he texted me saying he wanted to see me, to get back to good, I expect.

So when am I going to see you, babe?

I don't know. Saturday? If I stay at yours it's a shorter journey down to the boat on Sunday.

I may have walked away from the phone at that point, answered a call, even taught a lesson. Time blurs the detail, but I do remember there was a pause, a break in the conversation, and then I saw his reply and it made me feel sick.

Babe I'm out Saturday.

My heart pounded and my stomach lurched. Since my bad joke, the connection between us was breaking down and he had made other plans. I had brought this on myself. I replied with *"oh okay"* to let him know it wasn't okay, and that things were not good.

Things had now been less than good, less than bad even, for two long days. I felt paralysed, responsible for everything and incapable of fixing it without taking a trip back in time. I waited, because I didn't know what else to do, and to my relief and disbelief, on the Friday, Harry asked if we could forget it all and start over, because he missed me and loved me. The searchlight was back on. Curious detective had made way for a grateful doormat. He said he couldn't live like this, couldn't live without me, needed to see me, and he came over, taking me in his arms and holding me so tight it hurt.

"Are we good, baby?"

I was fighting back the tears. I wanted so much to say yes.

I left the children money for a delivery pizza, and told them Harry and I were going out. I had occasionally reminded him he hadn't actually taken me on a real date yet, and this time he had responded with a huge bouquet of amaryllis and a choice of two activities.

"I thought we could go and sit on the common in the sunset and have a picnic."

I had driven past all the loved-up sunset picnic couples a few days before, and I wanted to be them, with memories of lying on our horse jump sunbeds in Dorset soaking up the last rays.

"Or I will take you out for a meal. You choose. I just thought that a picnic, as it's so hot..."

The picnic idea won hands down. He ran down the road and returned with a Sainsbury's bag full of treats. Half an hour later we were lying on a blanket by the pond on the common, watching the sun go down and drawing a line under the week's events.

"Thanks for this, Harry". I gave him a tentative smile. It was getting cooler as the sun set but I steeled myself against the falling temperatures. This was not the time to complain about the cold.

He poured my wine and took his half of the blanket from under him, draping it around my shoulders. "Better?"

"How did you know?" I smiled.

"It's bloody freezing, that's how!"

We talked about Dorset. When things aren't right, it's instinctive to take yourself back to when they were, and we both did that well, recalling in impressive detail the moments when things fell into place, the number of coincidences about our past, the way things could have gone wrong at so many points. Harry reminded me of the night I spent with Isabel, calling him out on every failure to comply with my model of the perfect date. We laughed at how things had turned around. I closed my eyes and he dropped titbits into my mouth, poured me more wine and drove me home with a new smile on my face. We were good again.

CHAPTER 16

Touch and go

I woke up before it was light, vomiting and feverish. My head was pounding and cramps seared through my body, sending me to the bathroom where I spent an hour retching and clutching my tummy in agony. Harry brought me water, left me to sleep, tidied the kitchen, emptied the dishwasher, kept me informed of everything as it happened. It was nearly eleven when I opened bleary eyes to see him silhouetted in my bedroom doorway, one hand on the door frame, slightly out of breath from climbing two flights of stairs.

"I'm waiting for the kids to wake up so I can make them an omelette."

Why he had decided on an omelette I was too sick to fathom. I tried to whisper that Sadie wouldn't want breakfast and Josh would probably prefer a fried egg sandwich, then drifted back to sleep. When I woke again in the afternoon, still blurry and dizzy, he had cancelled his night out. The one that had meant I couldn't stay at his house. There was no danger of me wanting to do that now.

“I’m going to stay with you babe. You need me here.”

But I’m never sick. Not with paralysing stomach cramps and a crashing headache. I have never known sickness like that. Harry sat on the bed with me and pressed a cold flannel to my burning forehead, until I moaned and staggered back to the bathroom. When I came back he had plumped up the pillows and smoothed down the duvet. I stroked his hand in gratitude and closed my eyes.

"There's washing to hang out."

"Don't worry about anything in the house. I'll sort everything. You take your time."

"Didn't you have to do stuff today?" I couldn't remember, but I was too exhausted to worry about whether this was yet another thing that had slipped my mind."

"There's a house I was going to look at in Putney."

"Go and see it. Take my car."

"You sure?"

I nodded and sank back into troubled dreams.

He was out for the rest of the day. The children tiptoed up the stairs, held my hot hand, stroked my head and looked at me with fear and worry I hadn't seen before. I murmured that I just needed more sleep. They asked what was wrong with me. I said I'd eaten something, or just caught some sort of bug, and we let it be. Alone in my bedroom, as the pain abated and the vomiting eased, I thought through what I'd had to eat and drink the day before, remembered Harry handing me my wine as I sat wrapped in a blanket in the sunset, and then later, tipping his away after I poured into his glass what I couldn't finish.

If I had any real worries at that moment, they were forgotten when Harry bounced back into the room, full of excitement about his house viewings. I was sitting up in bed sipping water.

"How you feeling?"

"Not too bad now. The worst is over."

"Thank God. You had me worried."

"So let's see then. Got any pictures?"

He showed me photos online of the place he had just viewed. It was a small terraced house just off Putney High Street with a garden and off-street parking. I flicked through the pictures, hardly able to focus, but forcing a smile.

"Are you going for it then?"

"I made an offer and they've already accepted, but I can't move in for a month."

"So what are you going to do?"

"Live at Mark's place."

"He okay with that?"

“He’s fine with it. I’m so pleased I’ve found something. And you can stay anytime, do your teaching from there. Look, you can use this.” He swiped back to a photo of a sun-drenched dining room where a Georgian bay window looked over a tidy lawn below.

“Thanks,” was all I could manage.

"Now where's that list of jobs?"

I suggested he could trim the hedge at the front if he felt so inclined, and he assured me it was the least he could do. I watched him from my window, bringing order to chaos, sweeping up the leaves and pulling weeds from the gravel. Pulling on a dressing gown, I ventured out to the front porch and handed him a beer which he accepted with alacrity.

It was touch and go whether I’d make it to the sailing trip the next day, but I rallied, and we went.

After an unpleasantly early start and an hour’s drive, we reached the river Hamble just as the sun was beginning to break through the cloud. Caro was already aboard, pulling out ropes and attaching them to things. Harry climbed on and joined in with enthusiasm that made me smile and feel proud, introducing himself to James, Caro’s university friend Rob, and another couple I hadn’t met before. It was one of those groups that instantly gels, and with them, Harry and I were a couple. Nobody asked how we had met, how long we'd been together, and that gave me a sense of relief.

It was perfect sailing weather, and once we had reached the open sea, our novice crew obediently shuffled from side to side with every tack, turning handles and pulling ropes when instructed. Harry took selfies against the backdrop of the waves, hooting with excitement at every roll and pitch, updating his WhatsApp picture and status to tell the world what a whale of time he was having. The excitement on his face was new. I hadn't seen him this on fire before.

"I'm definitely going to learn to sail." He declared as we docked at Cowes Marina. "That was the best fun I've ever had in my life." He proceeded to engage James in a conversation about the best courses, the best sailing holidays, and soon he was trying to persuade me to join him on this next venture. I made excuses, said I would think about it, and chastised him playfully for being so impetuous.

Wine was opened, baskets of picnic surprises were turned out onto the folding table and we tucked in to a feast of unlikely offerings, cinnamon muffins, smoked cheese, Pringles and raw carrot batons. Harry was the life and soul of the boat, chatting to the boys about cars and motorbikes, describing his work, the Seatseller app, and winning new friends left right and centre. I leaned in for another selfie and felt good and safe again.

We strolled around Cowes, stopping at a sweetie shop where I bought Harry bags of gobstoppers and lemon sherbets.

We had a drink by the river before driving back home – cocktails in the sunset for the crew with pizza to share - and agreed it would be difficult to imagine a more perfect day. Harry stood aside from us for a while, staring out at the estuary, and I went to put my arm round him. He asked me if I was okay. Of course I was, as long as he was. He said later he thought that there was something between me and Rob. I reassured him, but in my mind there was a voice saying that this was just Jealous Craig all over again.

Back home, the tensions that had preceded our sailing day set right back in. He left for work in the morning and as soon as we were apart, I felt disconnected from him and unable to articulate why. Our conversations on the phone were stilted. I was nervous, wanting to ask things but not able to. Harry would ask me over and over, *"What is it that happens when I'm away from you babe? You're panicking again."*

I couldn't answer, partly because I didn't know, but the little I did know, I couldn't express. He was at my house often enough, but when he wasn't, I was painfully aware that I couldn't place him in any context. He said he was staying at Mark's, now that his house had been emptied, and I knew better than to argue, because he would look at me as if I'd gone mad, or didn't trust him, which was worse.

"What's up with you baby?" It started me wondering what *was* up. I was becoming a wreck of insecurity, suspicious and distrustful with no reason.

"Nothing. Nothing at all. Ignore me," I said, and then there was a pause, and my stomach fluttered with anxiety. Wine calmed me, so I drank more wine. It helped me sleep.

He came back on Tuesday evening and I was safe again, but how soon until he left again? I didn't dare ask. I just made him dinner and sat looking into his eyes in the hope of finding the answer, but he just pulled his phone out of his pocket and put it to his ear. "Harry" he said, standing up and walking over to the French windows. I jumped when Josh came into the room.

"Mum, there's a problem."

He looked at Harry, then back at me as if to say *can you ask this loser to leave?* Harry walked out into the hall saying "I know. I told you that yesterday. Get with the fucking programme already." I looked anxiously at Josh but he didn't seem to have heard.

"What kind of problem?" My instinct was to jump to the worst conclusion, that he'd made someone pregnant, that he was coughing up blood, that he was going to run away to the circus, or more likely, the RAF.

He sat down at the kitchen table, spreading out a few sheets of typed paper, forms with post-its attached. I sighed with relief. This didn't look like a pregnancy situation at least.

"What is it?"

"It's about my work experience. I need to find something. The deadline is tomorrow for handing the forms in. Mr Marshall says I'm the only one who hasn't done it yet."

"Is that all?" I felt the tension rush from my body and pulled out a chair next to him. "It has been on my mind, but no response so far from the usual places. I put something on Facebook and LinkedIn, but nothing came back."

"I have asked a couple of friends at school. One of them has an uncle who might offer me something. He's got a few going already but there might be a chance for me too."

"Sounds good. So…?"

"It's just that it's not definite, and I need to put something down here."

Harry must have been standing within ear-shot, because he came in just at the right moment.

"I've got something, Josh, if you're interested?"

He looked up, taken aback, but smiled politely and said "What is it?"

Harry had two suggestions. Either Josh could work with Mr Dawson senior on one of his projects in town, or he could ask Mark Rathbone who had an IT firm in Putney. He said Mark did this sort of thing all the time and was always on the lookout for good coders.

Josh was delighted. Computer science was his favourite thing, after warfare and Boost bars, and the sound of the job, when Harry explained it, was music to his ears.

"I'll call him this afternoon. Should have an answer for you by tomorrow."

And this became another thing I asked about every day, just like the Spain tickets, whether he had contacted Belinda about the Dorset house in August, and whether there was any news on his missing laptop and wallet. Yes, the cards had been returned. No, he hadn't replaced the Macbook yet, and in a tone of characteristic familiarity, he was "waiting to hear back from Tabs about the house". As for the airline tickets – they were booked – didn't I trust him? I felt like a nag, muttering a chorus of reminders that I was on the brink of insanity.

CHAPTER 17

Anna

My birthday was the next one after Caro's, and despite not being a multiple of ten, equally deserving of celebration. It was something we all did well, have parties, get drunk, dance until the early hours, and I wasn't going to be the one to let the side down. By then I'd known Harry for a few weeks, in real life that is. Of course, to me it was more like six months and probably in some wild fantasy, the whole of my life. That's what it felt like. But I'm just saying that I am aware that it was only a matter of weeks since we'd met. I'm aware now anyway. It was the whirlwind of whirlwinds and my feet had barely touched the ground.

I spent the morning before the party on last minute beauty tasks and was having my toenails and fingernails painted simultaneously by some very accommodating therapists at my local salon, when Harry appeared in the doorway bearing gifts. The bouquet was stunning. Stargazers, delphiniums and pink roses, pussy willow and ferns exploded from brown paper tied with ribbon.

"Happy Birthday, gorgeous."

The therapists were suitably impressed. Harry and his Eastenders-style gangster charm had made another conquest. Marta wanted to know all about him, how we met, whether I was in love... I prevaricated, realising I didn't know, not only whether I loved him, but anything about him at all. Trusting him had become a daily challenge which I was finding harder and harder. She didn't mind. She thought he was perrrrfect, and assured me I was just being careful, and that maybe that was a good thing. After all, you never knew.

The party was a blast. Anna surprised me by coming home from university, friends popped up from the distant past as well as neighbours from the present, and we danced our socks off. I introduced Harry to Maddie who had had the misfortune of seeing Craig kicking off on one of his jealous rages at one of her dinner parties. She was delighted with Craig's sturdy replacement.

"He's a keeper" were her exact words, brushing my uncertainty, once again, under a magic carpet of happiness.

The crew, led by Maya, presented me with a gift voucher for a four day countryside retreat, amid great fanfare, and the DJ struck up a jolly version of Happy Birthday followed by *500 miles*, which had us all doing high kicks we'd feel the next morning in our hamstrings.

He drove us back to my house that night, having, he told me, avoided drinking too much at the event. I knew that because at one point I asked him to buy me a glass of wine and he said he didn't have his wallet on him. So he couldn't have drunk much. He had a few glasses when we got back though, and a beer the next day mid-morning followed by a bottle or so of wine over the rest of the day. I pointed out that other options were available, and he just laughed and hugged me, joking that everyone drinks all day on a Sunday, and I thought maybe they did. Perhaps I was the crazy one here.

It was about 8.15 on Sunday night when Maddie texted. She wanted to come round to talk about Chris, and I knew Harry would be more than fine with my friend coming over, so I invited her round. She refused a drink, but Harry got on with more wine, topping up my untouched glass. At about 9.45, Anna rang from Leeds. Maddie and Harry were engaging in animated conversation, so I took the call and stepped into the garden to talk.

I am not proud of the kind of mother I was that weekend. Anna had come home for my party and gone back to Leeds less than forty-eight hours later. I had spent a total of half an hour talking to her on her own, my eldest daughter I hadn't seen for five weeks, because Harry was there and I had woven him into my family so tightly that it was somehow good enough that when she got me, she got him too. She wasn't ringing to complain about that though, or not specifically. She had a message from Sadie and Josh who were at that moment shut in their rooms upstairs doing their thing, which I had told myself was normal teenage behaviour.

The sun had set an hour or so before and the garden was in darkness, lit only by the streetlights of London that never allow us to experience total obscurity. From outside, the kitchen was lit up like a ship at sea. I remembered my father using that expression back in the day, with the subtext of *I'm paying for all this electricity you know.* He would never complain directly. He preferred the imagery route.

I stood on the small terrace and leant against the heavy glass-topped table that was too big for the tiny space it occupied. It was another vestige of divorce, a reminder of when our bulging bank accounts used to buy bigger and bulkier things than were strictly necessary: a five-bedroom house with a hundred foot garden, a Ford Galaxy, a nine-man tent for those middle class camping holidays in Cornwall where the kids skip around in mini-Boden beachwear and the adults feast on Prosecco and olives in the awnings. If I had been myself, the true me, I would have sold that garden furniture and got rid of the car, become a hippie eco-warrior with a dash of Druid, but here I was languishing in a dull London suburb, clinging to stuff that wasn't me.

Harry sat framed by the glass in the back door, leaning back in his chair, stomach heaving over his jeans, undisguised by the crumpled pink shirt. He had been on the hunt for the iron the previous day, but I didn't seem to own one, so his efforts went unrewarded. Unaware he was being watched, he let me see him, the real Jonathan Dawson; I examined him as one would an exhibit in a museum, and listened to the audio guide narrated by my observant daughter.

"Are you okay?" were my first words. It was unusual for my children to pick up the phone at all these days. They preferred messaging, texting, anything but making direct contact.

"Yes I'm fine, sorry, I should have texted first, to check you were free and stuff."

"Not at all." I glanced back at the house where conversation appeared to be ongoing and animated. "Harry and Maddie are here but they're fine." I felt a wave of uncertainty pass over me, the way you do when things are off-kilter. I wanted them to be friendly, civil, but not too friendly. I wanted them to miss me, glance out of the window occasionally, not be so wrapped up in each other. I felt awkward going back in. Their lips murmured words I couldn't make out over the rumble of traffic and the ambulance siren that came and went, changing its tone to longer and deeper as it passed. Something to do with Physics, the reason for that must be. I willed for silence to fall so I could catch their words.

"How's Maddie?" Anna was reading my mind from hundreds of miles away.

"Fine, as far as I know, why do you ask?"

"She always worries me a bit. It just unnerves me I suppose, how incredibly lively she is."

"I know what you mean, but there are plenty of reasons for the way people are the way they are. Maddie had a terrible childhood, abandonment, abuse, all of that, and she has never had a marriage or a proper family, just a son who has left home to live with his dad, who Maddie never lived with at all. I imagine life is pretty exciting once you have escaped all that horror. She is free and loving life, I'd say."

"What about the stuff that happened with you two?"

"Oh Anna, that was nothing, honestly, and ages ago. All water under the bridge, forgotten, done and dusted."

"But she told everyone stuff about you."

"I know, and she had her reasons, at the time."

"Did she though? I mean, was it true, what she said?"

It felt as if I stopped breathing then. I was at a crossroads, with cars hooting behind me. Decide. Decide. But I just pulled over onto the verge.

"That doesn't matter anymore, but it's not like she's holding a grudge. She's been a good friend to me. I like her a lot."

"What if she *is* holding a grudge, biding her time? I mean I feel bad now for saying it, but I just worry about you, that's all. I don't want you being friends with people who aren't your real friends. It's what you always say to me. Be true to yourself."

I took a breath, ran my fingers through my hair and stared up at the stars. How wrong this was, this role reversal where my own daughter was playing the parent. I wanted to look into her eyes an let her know she didn't need to worry, that teenage fanciful thinking was worlds away from the reality I lived in.

"Anna, you are a lovely, kind girl and I am so, so lucky to have such a caring wonderful daughter. I care about Maddie, I really do, and she deserves to have what she wants in life."

"As long as it's not your life that she wants."

I took that in, then brushed it aside. "I'm sure it's not that dramatic."

"But I worry, Mum, about you. Not just because of Maddie. There's something else."

"Go on, Anna, what is it? Tell me." I could tell there was something difficult, awkward to articulate. The pause was too long. I felt her pain, hated myself for causing it.

"The thing is, I mean this is a bit awkward to say, but..."

"It's fine Anna. You can say anything. Absolutely anything at all."

I felt my stomach turn over in dread, just as it had done after my misplaced message to Harry the other morning. I reminded myself that I was the parent here, that my responsibility in life, first and foremost was to her, Sadie and Josh.

So I listened. I listened without judgment, and with newly learnt humility, almost an eagerness to adjust, whatever the cost, to what she needed me to be.

Anna is an exceptional girl, woman I should say. Other parents have never ceased to marvel at how as a parent I dodged the torture that can be inflicted by teenagers during their adolescent years. Instead of rejecting me, retreating to a place of hedonistic self-obsession, feeling the world was against her and punishing everyone for it, she has always been there like an old soul, accustomed to this earth and the nature of its inhabitants. Anna would routinely get up and clear the table after meals, offer to walk the dog, smile at guests and ask how they were, and cut through any bad feeling in the house in the name of peace and harmony.

But such a personality is not without its issues. She also suffered from anxiety, even before anxiety became the buzzword it is today. All that giving takes its toll. Adam and I have had to remind her to put herself first, to value her own well-being before tending to the needs of others. Just like the lifejackets and oxygen masks on a plane. Put yours on first or you're no use to anyone. It’s not that I practise what I preach, but I have read the books, seen the Facebook posts, and the mantras are there, ready to be relayed at the first sign of dysfunction in others. Do as I say, not as I do...

Sadie was more of a normal teenager, as they go, with little to no concept of self-denial and a relentlessly acquisitive streak. Her wardrobe bulged with clothes bought on a whim and paid for by me to ingratiate myself with her swinging moods, and very few of the items were on hangers. Most were just stuffed wherever they could fit, pants still inside trousers, tops living in jumpers, and amongst them, plenty of things which weren’t clothes at all, theatre programmes, make-up brushes and things she didn’t know what to do with, like A level Physics revision guides.

Josh was the perfect little brother to those girls, dealing with their differences, treading on whichever eggshells they chose to place in his path, and above all, asking for nothing more than a few thousand calories a day and some bigger shoes, longer school trousers, on an alarmingly regular basis. One day he may reap the benefit of having sisters, having learnt to be bossed about but still carve his own path regardless. I was definitely guilty of trying to protect him from the world, and this probably delayed his development in some key areas. He would regularly oversleep on school days, lose his phone and forget his Oyster card, and I would step in and rescue him, because if he needed me, he wouldn't be able to leave.

Anna's struggle to get her words out was painful to both of us. She was between a rock and a hard place. Speak out and she would hurt me, but stay silent and there were other consequences. I said what I could to reassure her that whatever it was, I could take it, and however difficult it was to say, I would listen and do the right thing. Then, finally, she came out with it. She told me in an apologetic, half laughing, disjointed way that "It had all been a bit soon", that "It's nothing personal about you or Harry, nothing like that" but that Sadie and Josh wanted their space back. They wanted their house back.

I unstuck myself from the table, walked in circles on the pebbles that bordered the terrace and digested her words, holding the phone tightly to my ear as buses roared past on the road behind. Instead of drowning her out, the traffic reinforced the message, amplifying the disquiet that was being so eloquently articulated. Sadie and Josh didn't feel comfortable about the amount Harry was staying over. They wanted me to do something about what had for them become a new and unwelcome status quo. I gave Anna my assurance I would act on it.

"Thank you," I said. "Thanks so much for telling me all this. It must have taken a lot of courage to say, so thank you thank you thank you." I didn't add "for telling me *what I already knew*".

I stepped back indoors, shutting out the traffic, and Maddie and Harry barely looked up from their conversation. I stood a second until Maddie's inquiring glance prompted me to speak.

"There's a problem." I said.

Harry frowned and put down his glass. It was empty, so he reached for the bottle and unscrewed the lid, slowly, his eyes fixed on me. There was a glug glug glug as he spoke.

"It's the kids isn't it?"

"Yes." I said

Maddie's eyes opened wide. "What is it? What's wrong?"

When I remember that moment, it dawns on me that I may not have been able to confront him without the support of my friend. In our previous conversations about children, he had always been the perfect gentleman, assuring me that they would always come first, and now, as I explained that I needed to go upstairs and talk to them, he reiterated that he would do whatever was necessary, go now or whenever was needed. But I don't think he expected an immediate eviction.

"It's nothing, well it is something," I stuttered.

"It's me," said Harry, pouring his wine, lifting the glass to his lips, eyes still fixed on mine. I turned to the door.

"I've got to go and talk to them." I said.

Josh was rational, slightly embarrassed, but in agreement that the situation wasn't really ideal. I offered him the option of Harry leaving tonight or tomorrow morning, and he didn't choose the latter option, so I inferred that the other was the answer. With Sadie, it was a question of walking in and apologising for overlooking her needs, for ignoring what I think I must have known at some level, which was that whatever benefit, whatever fairy dust love, cooking and dishwasher stacking Harry was giving me, this wasn't a benefit felt by her, and I acknowledged that his presence in the house had been too much, assured her that he was going to leave now, and that things would be different.

She was tearful then, and cried more as we sat around the kitchen table with hot chocolate I didn't want but which seemed like a symbol of our reunion. My heart was doubly broken, first by Harry's swift and cold departure and then all over again by the realisation of what I had done to my daughter.

CHAPTER 18

Tuna

Before we reached the hot chocolate stage, there was some drama.

Getting Harry out of the house was no mean feat.

"Can I just finish my wine?"

"No. You need to leave now." With the added strength provided by a silently supportive, still wide-eyed, disbelieving Maddie, I looked him in the eyes, a lioness protecting her cubs, suddenly completely without fear, without guilt. I went and collected his things from upstairs, I hugged him, thanked him for understanding. He stiffened and withdrew.

"Where am I going to go?"

I thought it was obvious. He had assured me Mark was fine with him using the flat until the new house was free. It was my turn to frown, but Maddie spoke up right on cue.

"I can take you to Putney if you like, no

problem."

He hesitated, patted his pockets, looked around the room.

"I can't find my wallet." His eyes challenged me, accusing me of things he couldn't articulate.

I took the chance to escape, darted around the house looking for something I had never actually set eyes on, and returned empty handed.

"I must have left it at the golf club last night. Why don't you go via there then, on the way? I'm sure it's still open but I can check."

"Have you got any cash?"

The words grated on me, but I produced twenty, then another twenty, and a ten from my purse, waiting for the approval light to go on. He put the notes in his pocket, his eyes no longer in touch with mine.

"I'm sorry about this," I said.

"Don't worry babe," he said, turning away. "You gotta do what you gotta do."

It was around eight the next morning that I woke up to the ping of a WhatsApp message. It was Maddie saying that he had come back to hers in the end because he had lost his keys to Mark's as well as his wallet. They had stayed up till four in the morning drinking and talking. My stomach somersaulted. *Why talking? What about?* I pushed hard for answers but she was half asleep and didn't know if he was awake. My imagination raced. Was he in bed with her? Fury and jealousy surged through my body, reaching every extremity in a millisecond. I had been betrayed.

It took several rings for his blurry hungover voice to answer my call. He said he'd been for a drink in Putney having realised he had no keys, didn't want to bother me, asked Maddie instead. No mention of the fact they had been for the drink together, that she had offered her house when he had said he'd just sleep on the street. He was sweetening it for me, which I found simultaneously endearing and sickening. I calmed myself, knowing any jealousy would arouse anger I could do without, but it was simmering there anyway.

"I was angry, to be honest babe. I was angry."

"About what?" My heart began to pound. I sat down on the edge of my bed, fear mounting inside me, my legs beginning to shake.

"The way you sent me away. It was rude. I had no time to sort my stuff out. You were handing me my clothes. I couldn't even finish my drink."

"But I thought you understood. You said it was okay, that you'd do whatever was needed."

"Yes but that was no time, baby. I had no time. I had no wallet, no keys."

"Where are they? I thought you were going back to the venue to look for them? I rang them.

They were still open, waiting for you. Didn't you go and check?"

"I don't know babe. The thing is about me, I stash things. It's from when I was a drug addict. I hid my valuables and it's a habit I still have. I put things in places I think I'll remember and then I don't. You must have noticed that about me. I lose things." He used the word "me" a lot.

"Where do you think they are?" I asked. "I've looked everywhere, but I'll look again."

"In your house somewhere. I don't know. In a shoe, in something, not on something. Try your bathroom. Top shelf."

I looked while he was still on the line. Nothing there. It didn't make sense.

"But I don't understand. Why didn't you go back to the party venue?"

"What's going on baby?"

He had deflected my question again, but this time, without thinking, I went back with a swift reply I regretted.

"I don't know. You tell me."

"I love you, you know that don't you?"

"Harry..."

"Are we good? Are you and I good?" It was chorus time again, but I wasn't ready for the chorus. I wanted clarity, and here we were again, like interviewer and politician on the Today programme. I couldn't let it go.

"Just answer me. Why didn't you go and look at the club, in case you left it there?"

I knew it was futile, but I owed it to myself, to my imaginary radio audience, to try just once more. He caught the ball and threw it right back at me, in my face this time.

"You know, it sounds like there's something else going on here to me. I can tell by your voice, there's something you're not telling me."

I paused, reflecting on the irony of that, but knew better than to pull him up on it.

"There is nothing going on. Nothing with me anyway," I said, and hung up.

When Josh came in, I was texting Maddie a reply to her four messages that had arrived during the call. It was going to be a difficult balance to strike. I needed her support here and wasn't going to reveal her as the source of my information about him in case he stopped talking to her, which would block my channel of information. I needed to know that she was on my side. Like me, Maddie had an instinct to rescue waifs and strays. I needed reassurance that our friendship took priority over that, that I was the one in need here, not him.

"Is everything okay?" Josh looked sheepish, standing in the doorway. "Have you had an argument?"

"You could say that." I turned and reached out for a hug, which he gave me gladly.

"What about the work experience thing he promised?"

"I guess we'll have to see what happens. Can you ask the friend at school with the uncle?"

"But Mr Marshall...."

"I'll chat to Mr Marshall, Josh. Let me see what I can sort out."

Maddie came to my house later that day unannounced, on the pretext of visiting her son at his father's house. She breezed into the kitchen and heaped a pile of textbooks on the table, and a random can of lager, and I shut the door to give us privacy. Her eyes darted around the room, her hands were restless, moving over the objects in front of her, then onto her lap and back onto the table. Her mouth twitched, as if trying to smile, but not quite managing. I looked at her, not knowing what to think, how to be, or who she was anymore. Anna's words echoed in my head and I batted them away, but they couldn't be unheard now. Maddie tried to explain, in stops and starts, what was going on, why she was there.

"I told Harry I was taking Seb his books. I had a whole fake phone conversation where I pretended he was asking for a beer as well. I even said to Harry should I take him a beer and he said yes why not."

I sank into a chair and picked up a psychology revision guide, making a mental note to read one of these one day for my own benefit.

"It's elaborate – but kind of sad that it's come to this. You can't leave your own house without the permission of a homeless fantasist alcoholic?" I said "homeless" without thinking, and the word hung in the air for a second, waiting to be shot down.

Maddie would always resist blanket condemnations of people, and has an answer for every pigeon-holing platitude. She would have made a good criminal barrister, bringing up positive character evidence to counteract assumptions of guilt.

"It's so difficult. He has spent the whole day sorting out my garden, moving plants and furniture, making it all look fabulous."

My ego made a mental note of that. *What he does for me, he does for everyone,* and my insides hardened in response as another layer of trust crumbled.

"What's he doing now?"

"He's in his room drinking. He just went out and bought two bottles of wine."

"*Two* bottles?"

"I know. He said it was bank holiday Monday, so why not..."

"Does that mean double drinking, like double pay on a bank holiday?"

"I guess for him, and maybe he's going through some stuff with you and it's an emotional response."

"I wish people could find other ways of responding to things."

"He was upset that you didn't get in touch last night, and then this morning you said you were good, but he's been pacing the floor like a tiger imagining all sorts of things."

I flinched at the implication I had any responsibility for his behaviour, and wondered again whether she was falling under his spell.

"What kind of things?"

She hesitated, looked down at the pile of books. "Like you getting back with Adam."

"That's just a fear left over from his last relationship. The mother of his youngest left him to go back to her husband." Suddenly I was an expert in psychology, as if the content of the revision guides had been automatically absorbed into my head just by looking at them.

"That might explain it. You know, I think his feelings for you are genuine. He really does care about you."

"What about the drinking? Do you think it's a problem?"

"Well he drank everything in my fridge last night, and this morning it looked like he'd been out to get some cans of JD and coke"

"With my money." In my mind I saw the cash passing from my hand to his as we said our goodbyes.

"With your money."

"Tell me again about last night?"

"I drove him to Putney and then he realised he didn't have his keys."

"You mean he *told you* he didn't have his keys."

"Okay he told me that. Actually, thinking about it now, I don't think he had them at all, ever. Anyway, he wanted to go for a drink. He said "*it's on Rachel*", but I had a soda water. He was angry about how you'd been towards him, said… Oh never mind what he said but it wasn't very nice."

"Tell me. I need to know." I didn't need to know, but it was part of going through the pain. *I want the worst to be over.*

Maddie took a breath and her words came out in a rush. "He said that it didn't matter because if you dumped him he'd have his balls banging someone else in a couple of weeks."

There was a pause as we both contemplated what she had just said. Revulsion and vindication – the bitter taste of triumph mixed with disgust.

"Or something to that effect."

It didn't matter, the words were out. I shut them inside the box of evidence, in case I ever needed reminding, and turned back to her, calm and ready. She didn't need to know how much of a betrayal this was, not just by him, but by her, not throwing her soda water in his face at that point. But to let her know that would mean never hearing the end of the story, never knowing how truly despicable this man really was.

"Okay, carry on." I steeled myself.

"So then he wanted to go for another drink somewhere else, but it was shut. He said he was used to sleeping rough, or he could get a hotel, but I offered him my place because, that just seemed like the right thing to do at the time. I know, that sounds awful, but I just offered without thinking and then it was too late. He came back. Cracked open some wine and helped me stalk Chris."

"Stalk Chris?" He hates stalking. Harry had told me in no uncertain terms that it wasn't normal looking someone up online. It was after my night out with Isabel – with her frighteningly accurate assessment of what I was letting myself in for.

"He's seriously good at it. But it all happened without me, like he was on some kind of mission. He set up a fake email address to send a message to Chris, guessing a whole load of different formats of his name, he did a Companies House search, loads of things. I didn't even want to do any of that stuff. He was going way too far."

My mind was eased at the news that the focus had been on a relationship other than their own. I thought *"you could have stopped him"* but I didn't say it. I could have stopped him long ago but I hadn't.

"What's happening now?" I asked.

"I don't know what his plan is."

I thought *"You could ask him. Hell, you could tell him the plan for Christ's sake,"* but I just said curtly "You've got to get him out."

"I know, but I don't know what to do, or what to say. He's done all that stuff for me in the garden, he's all jolly and thinks everything is hunky dory, well as long as you're texting him he does."

"Just ask him to leave." It was easy for me to say, but when our eyes met there was another message, from me to her, that the time had come to call a halt to this unspoken revenge game.

Maddie hung her head slightly, looked back up at me and nodded slowly, then checked the time on her phone.

"I've got to go." She stood up, gathering the textbooks into a pile again. "What shall I do with these? I'm supposed to have taken them to Seb."

"Leave them here? Or no don't, in case he comes back and sees them. Take them away. I don't want trouble."

"I'll hide them in the car. Have you got any food I can take back?"

"Food?"

"I mean, I've been out a while, I was supposed to be just popping round the corner. It's easier if I pretend to have gone shopping. Is there anything I can take back with me for him? A ready meal or something?"

We managed to find some baked beans and tuna, which Maddie seemed delighted with and she left in a flurry of panic, dropping books, picking them up again, coming back for her keys, struggling to put up the front I was used to seeing. And I felt a selfish wave of relief that this man wasn't my problem anymore, but a gnawing sense of loss, and a bitter cocktail of sadness spiked with jealousy.

CHAPTER 19

Hung up

When Harry sent me a message later that evening I texted him back that I was talking to Adam about the kids. I think he expected me to call him afterwards, but the truth was I wasn't talking to Adam about anything. I was watching a terrible film on Netflix with my teenagers and loving every moment of being with them. I knew Harry would be disappointed with no contact. But I was nailing my colours to the mast now.

Then later that night, doubts surged back into my consciousness. Was I wrong to ignore him? He was unstable. And now so was I. I should have had the conversation, not run away from it. We needed to sort things out, but I was terrified, because around the corner were recriminations and loneliness and that was an unbearable thought.

I texted Maddie on WhatsApp.

Has he gone yet?

When I didn't get a reply, but saw that she

had seen the message, my stomach churned with the conviction that things weren't as simple as I thought. He must have stayed over at her house again. There was more to it.

I woke at six, to see messages from him

Hey babe, just checking you're okay. I know you must be stressed. The only thing that matters to me is your happiness.

Tears rose in my eyes and I blinked them away.

And from her, long after midnight.

Harry stayed here again. Just going to bed now. He was super-respectful last night. He noticed me wincing and asked me about my neck pain. He offered to give me a massage, and did just neck and shoulders, through clothes, really loosened it up. I think he's sad you didn't contact him last night.

Now my stomach somersaulted in pain. First the moving in, the gardening, and now the massage, and the implication that I was wrong to ignore his message, that I should be there for him. My relationship with Harry was quickly becoming a joke, a broken record with a script that was just on constant confused replay without even a day's break. I read the message again, swallowed my pride and sent him a text.

Good morning, then *How are you feeling?*

Good. Why?

I had fallen at the first hurdle, letting him

know by the use of one unnecessary word that I knew he'd been drinking, and therefore that Maddie and I had spoken. Now she'd be in trouble for going behind his back. I tried to placate, but it came out wrong.

I was just asking how you were. Are you okay?

Okay Rachel, what's going on?

Before I could answer, the phone rang. I made a mess of the conversation, mumbling my insecurities about him staying with Maddie again and not telling me. I told him it wasn't okay to just move in with my friend, that I didn't know what to think, and that I was just upset, crying, feeling hopeless. Intermittently I threw out accusations.

"You always said you'd stay with your mum if you couldn't get into Mark's. And you said you'd pay me the fifty pounds back into my account." I had already given him my bank details because he had offered to make a contribution to the bar bill at my party, but it had never materialised. That wasn't a sum I could call on as a debt, but the broken promise sat at the back of my mind and fuelled my anger now. Yet despite myself, I floundered like a fish on the deck, gasping for air, unable to control what I was feeling or saying, unable to communicate with the man with whom I had such a "connection".

As I stumbled over my words, his became more violent. Why hadn't I called after speaking to Adam? Was there something going on I wasn't telling him? I fumbled for excuses. I said I was trying to deal with the fact he was so angry about leaving my house, when all I was doing was the right thing by my children.

"You said you understood," I pleaded, "you said you knew my kids came first and would do whatever was needed to respect that."

"You don't think I had a *right* to be angry? After you give me absolutely *no notice*, no *time* to sort myself out?" Then he was telling me about how different Maddie was from me, and how I needed to take another look at myself and my behaviour not just towards him but to her.

"Sounds like *you* haven't always been the ideal friend, Rachel, so before you throw any more stones, think about glass houses."

I was shocked into silence, so he carried on. "You say you're loyal, you're always taking the moral high ground aren't you? But you don't mind stabbing your best friend in the back. She's the kind one here. She wouldn't throw me out on the street with no warning."

He would have talked for ever, but I felt the cords around me tightening. It was now or never. I hung up. And I never hang up because it's never the answer.

His answer came straight back,

I can't do this anymore, and as for my *disgust-*

ingbehaviour... it seemed that words could not express the extent of his revulsion.

Meanwhile, there was a message from Maddie, a screenshot of his message to her.

"Can we talk Maddie? Now?"

She texted me. *Wish me luck.*

Other online messaging platforms are available, obviously, but WhatsApp is a wonderful thing, if you know how to use it right, and that day, Maddie, as if she knew exactly how much I distrusted her at that moment, used it just right. Sitting at her kitchen table with him, she pressed the microphone button, holding it down for the duration of her conversation with Harry, and coughed discreetly to disguise the ping as it winged its way over to my phone. I heard everything. How he hadn't even done his *10 minute wait rule* before ending things with me, that clearly I wasn't being honest with him, that I obviously had a history of dishonesty, I was hiding something, and that there was no turning back for him now.

"When my head's gone, my head's gone."

He didn't want her to tell me about the massage incident.

"She doesn't need to know about stuff like that." Stuff *like* that? My insides turned over with horrific visions of them taking things to the next level, tearing each others' clothes off, fucking like

animals. I dragged my mind out of the gutter and rewound to hear his words again.

"That was her fault. She should have picked up the phone to me. What does she expect? Of course I'm going to look elsewhere."

So the massage happened because I hadn't given him the low-down on the Adam conversation. It was some kind of punishment for not talking to him when I should have. I was now, finally, witnessing Harry in action, justifying his every move, weaving his web of lies and planning its dissemination. His final words made his intentions clear.

"If she ever gets in contact again, she's in a battle zone with me. I won't soften on this. It's not good. I'm not good when I'm angry." Maddie asked questions, then let him rant, like an interviewer waiting for exactly the right soundbite.

"She's going to regret messing me about." Then, *"And she's messed you about before, hasn't she? I mean, this girl's got form."*

"I wouldn't say that." Good, I thought, because right now bringing that up feels like the last straw for me.

"She stole your man, didn't she? She's a lying conniving bitch. Why the fuck are you friends with her? Waiting for your moment of revenge? Is that it?"

"It wasn't like that at all." Maddie's voice was louder, insistent. *"You're blowing things right out of*

proportion. That is nothing to do with where we are now. You need to make a decision about where you're going."

There was some muffled chat after that, before the final cough. I sat in stunned silence for a minute, taking it all in.

I was struck by the irony of it all – remembering him letting me overhear his conversation with Nicky a few weeks previously. I am a fly on the wall again, but this time he's the one sounding off in ignorance.

"For an app developer, he's not very savvy," Maddie said afterwards.

CHAPTER 20

Tuesday

I was single again, dumped from a height by this man who was not what he said he was, and now I had had my fate confirmed by his voice, preserved forever on my WhatsApp chat.

Instead of taking some time to process this, my instinct was to dig in deeper, strengthen my position and answer the questions that still haunted me from the four weeks that we had spent in each other's company.

Had the packers ever come?

Was there really a new family moving in?

I texted Caro, who was, like me, all about the rules, but not as much about breaking them. She would be very concerned by a scam. She would also do a good job of going undetected, because she would never let herself get implicated in anything. Most importantly, she loved a good thriller, and being a part of one that was "live" so to speak, was a very exciting prospect indeed.

"Agent Holland, I have a mission for you, should you choose to accept..."

And she accepted with delight and enthusiasm. A little diversion to interrupt the torture of half term with primary school children. She sent me back photos of the house, the cars in the drive, ornaments in the window.

"It's definitely lived in."

"Yes, and normally that wouldn't mean anything – I mean he said there was a family moving in."

"So, does this tell you anything?"

I zoomed into the photo of the front door, where behind the stained glass the ornaments were just visible. I remembered the ones in the photo I had taken on my paranoid visit a few weeks earlier and they were identical, not a thing out of place.

"It does, Caro. It tells me the same people are living there as before."

"Oh my God Rach. What are you going to do?"

"I can't do anything. How can I prove anything? He would say that's the family living there."

"No photos from before, from when you went there last time? Can't you say you know nobody new has moved in?"

"I didn't think to photograph everything. I wanted to believe him."

“Sounds like you've had a lucky escape.”

“I suppose so.” But I felt incredibly, unbelievably cheated.

Harry texted me to say he was on his online banking app.

How much do you think I owe you?

I had added to the 50 the cost of our day out in Putney plus the odd twenty and fifty pound notes I had "lent" him. No mention of what he had cost me in food and wine just living in my house for the last few weeks.

How do you get to that figure?

Just pay me what you think is fair.

I hated this confrontation already.

Fair? Well that will be nothing then, in fact I might send you a bill.

I met Maddie and Jess at Ruby's. They expected me to be at least a little heartbroken, but I wasn’t. The trust had gone, and with it, every declaration of love, every promise, every kindness that had passed between us. I showed them the photos Caro had taken. Maddie was adamant that I had dodged a bullet. Jess was just as convinced I had stumbled upon a troubled soul with a good heart. She looked at me doubtfully.

"Are you absolutely sure that these are the same ornaments as the ones you saw?"

"Of course I'm sure. I'm not imagining this." I felt cornered.

"So where is he now?" she asked Maddie. "Not still at yours?"

"He's gone home to get his medication, in my car." She trailed off, suddenly thoughtful.

"In your car?" Jess asked in disbelief.

"It was going to be *my* car," I said, "but seeing as I'd thrown him out…."

"Which home are we talking about?"

"Godalming, he said."

"But he doesn't live there anymore. Or so he says."

"He said he had to inject his meds every day and he had run out so he had to drive down and get them."

"Every day? He told me every month."

"Well there we go. But he was really anxious to let me know where he was all the time. He called me to say that there had been an accident on the M25 and he would be late." She paused, bit her lip. "Should we check the traffic reports?"

"You don't go on the M25 to Godalming from here, more to the point," said Jess.

"But you might use it to go to Sunningdale."

"Sunningdale?" The girls looked at me, and I realised that I hadn't shared my last bit of research yet, and I needed to share it all, just in case.

"It's about this company, Hasam. It's named after Harry and Sam. Harry said Sam was the "bloke I set it up with" but in fact the two founders and initial shareholders were Harry Dawson and Samantha Brize. And the company's first registered address was in Sunningdale."

"So that must be where he went." Maddie was the one to jump on the hypothesis and go from there, leading us down a flow chart of conjecture which at every turn had a 50:50 chance of being right. Or wrong.

"Are you thinking she's his wife, and they're still together?" asked Jess.

"Anyone's guess, like everything else."

There was a respectful silence, the kind you expect when you tell your friends you have staked your entire fortune on the horse that fell at the first jump.

"I don't want him back, but I have loads of his stuff at my place."

"Me too," added Maddie.

We sipped our coffee, thoughtfully, occasionally bursting out with an idea.

"I know, why don't we take his stuff down to the house in Godalming? I could just knock on the door, explain the story." It was a long shot, I realised as I said it.

"To some random family?"

"There's no family moving in, we've established that, and I'm pretty certain from the land registry search that his mum lives there. She might even tell me the truth."

Jess nodded. "You could do that, but take someone with you maybe? Just in case?"

"What about taking it all to Putney? To the guy he's supposed to be staying with, Mark," offered Maddie

"You wanna do that, Maddie?"

"Sure. Anything." Sadness flashed across her face, just for a second.

"How did we get here again?" asked Jess, to nobody in particular.

How we got there I don't know, but I'm beginning to understand myself because of it. I thought I was a good detective, but a little more curiosity at an earlier stage might have led me somewhere different. My biology teacher once said that I didn't have an enquiring mind, and he was right. I am no scientist. I am vaguely aware of some basic laws of physics but the rest of it, from how a kettle boils to the sun rising and setting, I have always secretly attributed to a kind of magic that for me preserves the wonder of the world. I let things happen, and only when the whole vessel capsizes do I go into investigatory mode.

With a little more forethought, so much of this subsequent unravelling could have been avoided. Eat cake now, worry about it later, then go into workout overdrive. I never questioned Harry about where he really lived even after it became clear he was lying, I never asked him to show me the Seatseller app on my laptop (after all, it was all on the cloud apparently). I never saw a picture of him *with* his dog, just the dog on its own on Tinder, which could have been a stock internet picture, I never met any of his friends, or heard the buzz of his office in the background when he was on the phone. I never saw his wallet or his keys. I picked him up and dropped him off at stations, accepted invitations to go on holiday, took his word for everything. At the bottom of it all was my need for it to be true, my wilful blindness to the possibility that it wasn't. I had told him what I wanted, and he had given it to me. But it was never his to give.

CHAPTER 21

Wednesday 31 May

I lay in bed for an extra hour and focused on the days that lay ahead. I was supposed to be travelling to Spain with Harry the next day. I wondered what would have happened if things hadn't gone the way they had, if I'd let him stay, or had made up with him when he went to stay with Maddie. Tomorrow I'd be told *sorry there's been an emergency babe, we're going to have to postpone the trip.* Because it was never going to happen. He had never shown me the tickets, had probably never bought them.

But things had gone this way, and now I had a day to decide what to do with the long weekend of freedom that lay before me. My priority was to get away from London, somewhere he would never find me.

Then I remembered the voucher the girls had given me for my birthday. It was for a little place called the Hideaway, a farm cottage stuck out in the wilds of Dartmoor. From the website I gathered that it was populated mainly by artists and writers, but the emphasis was on peace and seclusion. I called the number on the website, not imagining for a second that there would be a place for me at such short notice. As it turned out, there were no bookings at all as a large group had just cancelled.

"So you are more than welcome, if you don't mind being on your own there. Susan can let you in and she'll just be around the corner if you need her.

I didn't mind at all. In fact I relished the prospect. I packed a bag, feeling the nerves twisting my stomach in knots as the phone pinged incessantly.

Harry was on the warpath. The messages were erratic, badly spelt, alternately showering me with venom and adoration, vitriol and victimhood. He accused me of lying, of unimaginable dishonesty. I appeased him in a roundabout way, agreeing that I had been dishonest, about the fact I didn't trust him when it came to his home, Mark's flat, the Sam part of Hasam, his team of developers, the app, the Spain tickets, booking Belinda's house, his promise to order wine for the party and pay back the money he owed me. And then he replied *thanking* me, and that he could prove all those things to be true. I wobbled. He saw my uncertainty and ran with it, repeating how much he loved me, that all he wanted was for us to be together. I wobbled again and steadied myself.

Then there was the small matter of Josh's work placement. I had seen Mark Rathbone on Facebook, easy to find with the information I had. In fact, the whole Dawson clan was easy to find. Harry's father was prolific in his posting, and through him I found the mother, stepfather, stepmother, children, sister, stepsister and step-brother, and almost all of them were somehow connected to Mark. Mark himself was a handsome Essex boy, with a laid-back smirk and aviator shades. He oozed money and fast cars.

I bit the bullet and sent him a message on Facebook.

"Hi Mark, you don't know me but a friend of yours suggested that you might be able to offer work experience for my son who is looking for a week's work from 26 June. No worries if not poss but just thought I'd follow up."

The reply was almost instant. He told me the office was in Putney and could Josh get there easily. We closed the deal.

"That sounds fine. Give me a call Friday." I put a reminder in my phone to call him. It was like having a present to open in two days' time. So much would come together once I had spoken to him. Mark Rathbone was the gateway to the truth when it came to Harry Dawson's real life. And there would be no more wobbles because I would

have my certainty at last.

There was only one thing left for me to do before I left. I gathered his possessions and drove them round to Maddie's house. She had a new plan which was to leave his belongings with a neighbour and join me on the retreat at some point over the weekend. There were various messages between her and Harry as he changed his plans and his methods for collection, but she stuck to her guns and wasn't going to be in the house, at any cost, when he or the courier arrived.

As I set off for Devon, Harry spotted my WhatsApp status had changed to "*rien de rien...*" and jumped on it, sending me the Edith Piaf video on YouTube and more poignant messages about how he missed me, needed to be holding me. I melted at his words, regretted everything I had said or suspected and wanted nothing more than to turn the clock back and comply, believe. I pulled into a layby to reply to him. I told him I understood, but I needed some time to think.

Then, just as I softened, he flipped again, telling me that I had sabotaged this relationship like I sabotaged everything. I said maybe I should reflect on that and sent him Peter Skellern's *Put out the Flame.* I needed him to stay peaceful as long as possible. I told him I was going to stay with a friend for the weekend, and a few minutes later he was asking, apologetically, whether I was alone. I sent him a laughing voice recording as I drove down the A3 "*of course I'm on my own, yes, I'm on my own,*" and he said how lovely it was to hear my voice, and apologised for his burst of jealousy, said it wouldn't happen again. He didn't mention the fact that we were booked on a plane to Spain the following day.

When he was calm, I was calm. When the temperature of our messages went up, I stressed and smoked. That was the pattern he had me in, like the old tennis game on the very first Atari in the eighties, I was constantly moving to catch the next ball. I never thought to let it go past, because I was afraid, I still don't know exactly what of, but he had me. He still had me. To extricate myself, to stop myself falling headlong back into his trap, I needed to remind myself that none of it was true. On a sudden whim, I took the Godalming turn-off. I needed to pay whoever really lived in that house another visit.

I don't know what I expected to find or do when I got there. When I arrived, I parked around the corner and walked back and up the drive to the front door. The ornaments were still on the windowsill, and photo frames were visible on the sills in the upstairs bedrooms. Two cars were in the drive, the Peugeot I'd seen before and the convertible Beetle which he had said belonged to his mother. The love cushion was no longer on the back seat of the Peugeot, neither was the charger cable plugged into the dashboard, and a beige jumper was slung across the passenger seat. This car wasn't off the road, it was in regular use.

The doorbell rang unanswered. The house bore the hallmarks of a couple on holiday. Through the kitchen window I saw gleaming surfaces, an upturned washing up bowl and cloths hanging over the taps. The door from the hall to the TV room was closed. I opened the bins again, this time photographing the recycling. I had no idea why I did that at the time, but later that day I zoomed in and googled the headlines of the Telegraph to determine when the house had last been occupied. A week ago. It was half term. Harry's mother was a teacher. It all made sense.

Back in the car, I hand wrote a letter to Harry's mother and stepfather Daniel and Jo, telling them who I was, and that I had met and had a relationship with their son Jonathan, who I knew as Harry. I told them we had split up because he had lied to me, that I didn't know why, that I had nothing to lose or gain now but was just curious as to what was going on and what was behind the elaborate stories I had been told. I tried to appeal to his mother on the sisterhood angle, but realised the motherhood issue might trump it. The letter was articulate, legible even, and amazingly the words flowed without any need for crossings out or asterisks. But even as I wrote it I knew I couldn't post it. I didn't have an envelope, and posting a piece of paper through the door left it open for anyone to read, and if Harry came by for any reason then I would be toast. I contemplated driving to a shop to buy an envelope, then I had a better idea.

The neighbours to the right didn't answer. The windows were open, cars were in the drive but they chose not to come to the door, for which I am grateful because that sent me round the corner. And that's how I met Julie.

She opened the door to me without hesitation. They say that when you set eyes on someone for the first time you make your judgement of them in seconds. Your decision to trust, like, love a person is made by your eyes and your heart in a joint venture of the soul. I looked at Julie and saw myself in her. She was my age, my height, and had an expression that filled me with hope.

"I'm so sorry to bother you, but do you have just a couple of minutes?"

There must have been a split second where she struggled to think of a single reason to say yes, and in that moment I managed to say a few more words *I know this sounds very odd, but I'm just trying to find something out, and it's to do with a scam and it's about one of your neighbours….* The words came out like bullets, clumsy, dangerous, scattergun. I looked at her with begging in my eyes and held out my hand tentatively.

"I'm Rachel by the way."

This seemed to put her at ease.

"I'm Julie. Nice to meet you Rachel. So how can I help?" She was holding onto the collar of a golden retriever with one hand, while the other held the door open. I still had something to prove, and the pressure to find the right words sent me stumbling over them instead.

"Thank you so much. I just wanted to ask, how well do you know your neighbours?"

"Daniel and Jo?" Not that well, just to say hello to, really.

"It's their house then, I mean they live there? Alone?"

"Yes, well, yes. Why?"

"They don't have a son, called Harry who lives there with them?"

She frowned and shook her head. "They have a son, Daniel's stepson, called Jonathan, who doesn't live there anymore, but I sometimes see him around when they're away."

"Oh yes of course, Jonathan, I forgot." That made sense. I wasn't imagining things then. "So do you know Jonathan?"

"He's done lots of odd jobs for me over the years. He put up some fencing here for me last Saturday." She indicated the boundary dividing her place from the neighbours.

"He did that for you? That's very kind and neighbourly of him."

"Well it's his job, isn't it?"

"Really? I thought he worked in the city? He told me..." I hesitated, wondering how much to divulge. "He told me he was an app developer, runs his own software development company in Liverpool Street."

Julie blanched visibly and her hand tightened on the dog's collar. "He's worked for the council as a gardener, since, well, I don't know..." Her voice drifted off. I was remembering Maddie talking about how he had sorted out her garden so *professionally*.

"Could you tell me anything else about him? Anything at all? It's just that I met him online, a few weeks ago, some stuff happened and I don't think he's – well, I think there is something very weird going on."

"Has he hurt you?" Her face suddenly clouded. The door opened a fraction further and I could see into the warm kitchen, where sunlight flooded in from the back.

"No, he hasn't been violent. Why, has he done that before?"

She glanced over her shoulder, through a side window which looked over the neighbours' garden. "Not that I really know about, or not exactly" she said, in a quieter voice. Do you want to come in?"

We chatted some more. I asked about the Mercedes and the motorbikes. She'd never seen him drive anywhere, not for a long time anyway.

Her hands twitched in her lap.

"There was an accident," she added, lowering her voice as if he might be there, waiting in the hallway. "Someone died."

"Oh my God." It took what seemed like an eternity for the words to sink in. My stomach turned somersaults. "Killed?"

"Terrible, I know."

"Who died?"

"I don't know. It was all very hush hush."

"He was drunk, and driving?"

"I don't know the details, but possibly, yes."

"Was he .... Is he an alcoholic, do you know?"

"When he came to the door to do the fencing the other day, I could smell it on his breath."

"In the afternoon?"

"About two thirty. Last Saturday it would have been. I think he could see me wince because he started apologising and saying he'd had a session the night before. And he was driving, I think. There was a car I didn't recognise. I remember being surprised at the car, given what had happened."

"That would have been my car. He borrowed it." To go to Putney, I thought. To see a house, he had told me.

Then I confessed to Julie, because I couldn't

confess to my children, that he had been driving us around for weeks, in my car.

We let that sink in, biting our lips, thinking the same thing.

“You said he hasn’t hurt you?”

“No, not yet, not like that, but…”

“Like what then?”

“It’s nothing, nothing that I can put my finger on. That’s the whole problem.”

“I think maybe steer clear of him, if you can.”

“I will. Thanks Julie.” I got up to go. We swapped numbers. I promised her I’d say nothing about what she had told me, and asked her not to mention my visit to anyone. Jo and Daniel might need a separate visit, but now the chasm between appearance and reality seemed so deep that I couldn’t imagine how to broach the subject. I tore up the letter slowly. What I hadn't mentioned to Julie, but what I couldn't stop thinking about as I drove away, was that I had recognised the golden retriever.

Back on the A303 heading south-west into the lowering sun, I passed Stonehenge again, a sturdy and constant backdrop to our hapless human exploits. I pulled over in a layby and closed my eyes, breathed and thought about peace. In the distance, tiny figures moved around the giant stones which stood rigid against the sky.

I remember visiting the site back in the seventies before the cordons and barriers went up. I hate barriers. I want to run through them and touch what lies beyond. I want what I can't have. How do you stop wanting what you can't have? Somewhere along the line we need to submit to higher authority, but with every bone in my body I want to break through it, make possible what isn't, find the truth, touch it, feel it.

The drive to Devon was uneventful after that, and I arrived at the cottage by nightfall, ready to unzip my laptop and finish marking some exam papers I had set for my students. But it was never opened. I procrastinated again. I blame that on what happened next.

"So there's Cathy and Jen tonight, when they come back from wherever they are, but they go tomorrow night, so you'll be alone after that." Susan, who managed the house in between retreats, was inching her ample body down the stairs in front of me, creaking in unison with the bannister. "Help yourself to anything in the fridge," she panted, easing herself into the kitchen, one hand on each side of the doorframe.

"Thank you I'll be fine. It all looks great."

"If there's anything you need, I'm just across the road, and here's my number." She pointed to a post–it on the hall table. "I'll be back in the morning to sort out the dogs, but don't worry, they have a dog flap, and they don't go upstairs." She pulled the heavy door shut behind her and I was alone for the first time in many weeks.

The cottage was as you might expect, thatched, low-ceilinged, with rooms that led to rooms that led to rooms. I set my things down on the floor in the hall, taking in the smell of wood-smoke and wet dog, the slow ticking of a grand-father clock. Two fat Labradors came wagging to meet me, then waddled back to their beds, tails still thumping, big brown eyes expectant. I stood there for what may have been minutes or seconds, just being still.

At some point Harry was going to know I had contacted Mark about the work experience, and if he hadn't managed to get there in time for my first message, it wouldn't be long now. It was Wednesday night. Mark said we could speak on Friday. I had 36 hours till I found out who Harry Dawson really was. And that still seemed possible, even as I finally drifted off to sleep at three in the morning.

CHAPTER 22

Thursday 1 June

I was woken at eight by the ping of WhatsApp. Messages arrived thick and fast, panicky, furious, vitriolic and reeking of revenge.

I know you emailed Mark. I know you've been going behind my back. How dare you contact a man who is basically family after what you have done to me? Have you absolutely no shame?

Then

You have no idea what you have set in motion here. Mark is going to know everything about you and your disgusting behaviour. You will be sorry.

The phone rang and rang until I blocked his calls and then he tried another angle.

Call me baby, just call me. I'll never stop loving you.

Then more declarations of love, getting more and more urgent, more desperate, and when I didn't reply to any of them, he sent me this.

If you don't call me, I'm on the warpath, and

when I am, I don't stop. You deserve everything you get.

Then, *I can find out where you are.*

It's the first day of June. I don't remember any other firsts of Junes, but I will remember this one.

The sun has set, the garden is in darkness. Cathy and Jen left an hour ago. I have double locked the front door and kept the curtains drawn tight.

There's a knock at some point but I stay quiet and whoever it is goes away. I breathe again, but I don't sleep.

The next morning I call Mark as we had agreed, but it goes to voicemail. Then he texts me.

"Sorry Rachel, I'm at A&E at Morefields Eye hospital. Will have to chat next week. My day screwed."

Whether it was threats, lies or violence, Harry Dawson had got to Mark Rathbone before he could tell me who this man really was. I never heard from Mark again.

CHAPTER 23

Friday 2 June

I took myself back to bed and stared at the ceiling. My mind raced with the questions I had wanted to ask - who is Jonathan or Harry Dawson? Does he own Hasam? Why is there no record of it online? Is he really developing a ticketing app for the FA? Who is Sam? Is Harry married? Do they live in Sunningdale? Why did he lie about the house? Does he have a car, a bike, a house in Spain? Is it true he is a gardener for the council? Is he homeless? Where does he live?

Where does he live? I had never actually asked myself that question. At some level I had been assuming he lived with his parents in their house in Godalming, but Julie had said he was hardly ever there. I went back onto Companies House website, where the registered office of the business was listed as his parents' house. Previously, and for one day only, it was listed at another house in the same road with a fake, or mistaken postcode. That address, it turns out, didn't exist. There was no number 74 on that road. The registered address before that, and the current correspondence address for Harry Dawson was listed as 5 Crossway, Sunningdale. The other business registered there was a massage therapist. There was no actual link between that business and Samantha Brize, the second shareholder of Seatseller. I still couldn't find any trace of Hasam. Seatseller Limited had no website or any other online presence, it had a share capital of £2 and had yet to file accounts. The FA had not bought shares in Harry Dawson's company. It was an empty shell, a hoax, perhaps a vehicle for a money laundering racket. But I had no proof of anything.

Dishonesty is a spectrum. At one end of it, we deceive ourselves on a daily basis about what matters. We choose Farrow & Ball paint, Nike trainers, and pay people compliments we don't mean so they like us and stay happy. We trick people into thinking we are thinner, richer, cleverer, funnier, luckier – just look at anybody's social media account. I am as guilty as the next person of projecting an image of myself I'd like them to have rather than who I am, warts and all. What if they didn't like the real me? Then I'd be abandoned again. But there is a difference between the universal dishonesty we all buy into in the west, and lying to extort money. That is a far less forgiveable kind of deceit.

Another message arrived. He wanted to

know how I was, because he was struggling and he wanted to know that I wasn't finding our separation easy. I resisted the temptation to tell him to look back at what he'd said, calling my behaviour malicious and disgusting, accusing me of lying to him and refusing to pay me what he owed, telling me he'd be sending a bill instead, threatening me that he was on the warpath. I didn't need to refer him to his own words. If he didn't remember them, or didn't understand their impact then I wasn't going to be the one to make that difference. Instead I told him I was numb, sleepy, confused, sad, that I wanted to shave my head and become a Buddhist monk, or shut myself in a dark cupboard. I had no energy any more. Everything I tried to do crashed and burned. It calmed him, as I thought it might. His WhatsApp picture changed again to a selfie of the two of us and he started asking again:

Do you still love me baby?

I didn't reply, and there were a few more, repeatedly asking *did I love him, did I*?

Eventually I told him I loved the real Harry, the one underneath all the lies and anger and fear. I said I had tried to pull him out but he seemed to want to stay there for now.

What lies? You disgust me.

Then later

I'm coming for you.

The picture changed back to Liverpool FC

and the status to "available". I felt that pain in my heart that you get when you hurt someone with bad news, when there's no other way to say it.

How's it going?

It was Maddie. I told her in blotchy summary what was going on, after deleting three drafts of it. I felt like a fraud, paranoid, obsessed. She asked if there was still a room in the house for her, and after checking with Susan, I told her *Yes, please, please come.*

There were lies, but Harry said I was imagining it, and every time he did, a part of me wanted to believe him all over again. Maybe I was wrong about all this. Maybe the house was actually his, and the move got postponed. Maybe he used to do some gardening before this app took off, and the alcohol on his breath was a one-off. Maybe he had booked Spain, rung Belinda, genuinely lost his laptop and wallet. I had no proof he didn't employ thirty people at his office in Liverpool Street. It was all still possible. He may well have been in a car crash, someone may have even died, but no-one in their right mind would drive on a ban. If you kill someone drink driving you go to prison, surely. I remembered my evening with Isabel, her insistence he'd been in prison, his denial, his story about hitting someone who deserved it. I wondered how often he had told that story. A quick internet search suggested that the maximum sentence for causing death by drink driving was 14 years, but that this was likely to increase to life imprisonment. Your sentence can be reduced by a guilty plea, or was that just for reckless driving? Surely drinking was drinking and death was death. How could pleading not guilty even be an option?

My head hurt with the tug of war between trust and suspicion. I needed more facts. I thought back to the day he had his laptop and wallet stolen. I couldn't remember the exact date, but looked up the Surrey police website and filled in a form asking whether there had been an incident reported and explaining why I needed to know. It must have flagged up something because an email pinged back a few minutes later saying that someone would be in touch.

I texted Belinda as well to see if she remembered ever actually getting the call from Harry about hiring the manor house again. I'd heard him make the call, but this would tell me whether that was another one-way conversation with nobody on the other end.

Now there was only sitting and waiting. I wondered how Mark was doing, what he was thinking, what Harry had filled his head with, then my trusting side kicked in and said maybe that was a genuine visit to the hospital, not provoked by anything at all on the part of Harry. Perhaps I was paranoid, suffering from some mental condition that made me perceive the world as my enemy. Maybe Maddie was in on this, fuelling my suspicions and egging me on to a place where I really would be locked in a dark cupboard with a bald head and orange robes, while she rode off into the sunset with my man. Harry said there was something wrong with me, that I had trampled all over him, us, our future. Maybe he was right. I sat still at the dining table, staring out at the square where a group of cyclists were consulting the village map before setting out on the next leg of their ride. They passed round a plastic bottle, gesticulating down the hill with grins and back slaps, exuding health and vitality. Watching them in the silence of the empty cottage, I felt drained of life, an empty shell with a broken heart.

My melancholy reverie was interrupted by the phone ringing. I looked at the screen. No caller ID. I ignored it. I didn't need Harry's wrath anymore. I was done talking to him. Every so often he'd say he was done as well, flinging finality at me before coming back for one last go, one last stab at getting me to hate him, love him, answer him, anything. The caller left a voicemail. Surrey police asking me to call 101 urgently for the purpose of "safeguarding myself". I decided that the best safeguarding available was right here in the village square, with the chain on the door and two fat Labradors for company. They were following protocol, I got that, but all I needed to know was whether a crime had been reported that day at Godalming station or not. I opened my email and the response to my query was that no report had been received, but that I should contact the Transport Police, which meant another email, which in turn generated a reply informing me that my enquiry had been passed to the data protection team. I cursed protocol. Everywhere I turned was more uncertainty. Everything pointed to lies but the level of proof hadn't been reached. Despite everything I knew in my heart to be a lie, there was still a sliver of doubt cutting through my case where Harry could slip through unscathed. I needed more evidence.

CHAPTER 24

Memories of a deleted proposal

Maddie arrived that Friday night. I was so happy to see her. I hadn't warned her about the shabbiness of our accommodation because there was a bit of a conflict, seeing as she had organized the joint present. To my amusement, she seemed just a little aghast at the sight of the boarding house set up in the dining room and the pervasive odour of mothballs that permeated the upstairs. It was all even more of a let-down after her torturous 5 hour drive during which the map app used all her phone battery, leaving her stranded at Exeter at the mercy of road signs and basic sense of direction, both of which were in short supply.

"My mother wouldn't be able to handle this." She looked around at the tupperwares of crackers and mini jam pots.. In the corner, the electric massage chair I had barely noticed looked suddenly jarringly out of place. And that was all she needed to say. I got it. It was good to have my friend back.

We ate salad and drank wine, not too much – we mustn't be alcohol hypocrites – and Maddie flipped open her laptop. She had been doing some digging as well.

"One thing that's been on my mind is this Sam."

"Samantha Brize of Hasam fame?" She had been on mine too. After all, I may have been sleeping with her husband.

"Yes, but there's something else." Maddie was adept at flipping open a number of tabs at once, so we had the whole Dawson clan on the screen and could flick between them like reports in a filing cabinet. Harry's friends were hidden, but Maddie looked up the people who had liked his profile photos.

And that's where she appeared. Sam Dawson.

"It could be another Sam, a cousin?"

"It could, but look, here are the cousins, you can tell if you follow the links and the family status, and she's not even on their list of friends."

"A random coincidence? Or she doesn't look at Facebook much? Or she's fallen out with them?"

"Always possible, but if we go down that route we go nowhere."

I didn't want to go somewhere just for the sake of it. And I didn't want any more lies to be uncovered. With each one I felt a new wave of self-doubt, followed by guilt, pity and shame at my role in this, and at my lack of trust. But Maddie was pushing this one. She looked at me, biting her lip.

"You're thinking he's married."

"It would make sense, he got married, set up a business with her, then they split up, and she is still a shareholder but not a director."

"But Harry hasn't been married."

"That's what he said, but he asked you to marry him after 2 weeks didn't he? So maybe she said yes when he asked her."

I wasn't kidding myself that I was the first person he'd asked. It was perfectly possible, and the more I thought about it, the more likely it was. Harry had asked me just last week. He was cleaning out my car while chatting to the neighbours, winning them over with his well-practised charms, and I brought them some beers. He asked me to marry him in between swigs, and then later he said,

"Actually, let's not get married. You don't want to get married again do you?"

I had forgotten it immediately, deleted it from my fairy tale, but Maddie had remembered. It was weird to change your mind about something like that so quickly. Unless of course you suddenly remembered you were already married.

There was a WhatsApp ping, and I glanced at

my phone. In the three lines of the message that were visible, he was telling me this was the last message I would get from him, and that it was my last warning. I swallowed hard, fought back a rush of tears that had sprung from nowhere, and looked back at Maddie's laptop. She had looked at the likes on Sam Dawson's handful of photos, clicked on the names of the likers and searched for more photos of her on their timelines. We found more Sams on LinkedIn, although most turned out to be men. By midnight we were flagging, and nowhere nearer the answer.

I was making us camomile tea to take upstairs, when I blurted out, without any sort of intention, "We're okay, Maddie, you and I, aren't we?"

"What?" She put her head on one side. "Of course we're okay. What makes you ask?"

I couldn't back out now, so I let the words step tentatively forward. "It's just that, with all the Harry stuff, you know, staying at your house. It crossed my mind, occasionally, that I might be missing something." She frowned, nodded slowly, and I took it as a sign to carry on. "You know. I've been so blind to the obvious recently, and if there's anything I need to know, please tell me, won't you?" I was stumbling now, thrashing around blindly in my clumsy attempt to reach out to her. *Reassure me* I was screaming inside. "I can't stop thinking about what Harry said in that conversation with you, about you wanting to get your own back."

I was regretting trying to say any of this, but Maddie just laughed. "Sorry, I don't mean to smile, or laugh. Of course I don't. But it's crazy to say that stuff. Of course there's nothing to know. I'm a hopeless liar, and what on earth would I see in some psychopath lunatic like Harry? I mean, give me some credit! And as for the past – it's the past."

And all I could think was that the more someone denies something, the more it's true. She was protesting too much.

"And you know it was a terrible mistake, and I'm sorry, and I was drunk, and..."

"It's forgotten."

I had dived into the murky lake and swimming to the other side felt easier than turning around. So I went on, and now it was me protesting too much. "I honestly thought, with what little thinking I was doing, that you and he were over, and that you had moved on, but I realise that I was making assumptions I had no right to make."

"Okay, have you finished now?" She looked me in the eyes but I couldn't tell what she was thinking.

"Yes, sorry, but this makes you crazy, never knowing anything for sure."

"I know. But you're not crazy."

And I believed her.

I was woken in the morning by the phone buzzing on my pillow. New Malden Police station had had an urgent message to contact me to establish my safety. I felt numb listening to the officer on the line, as she took a note of where I was, whether I was alone and when I would be back in London. I agreed to come to the station when I was back, but in my mind I was racing through possibilities: that Harry was known to police and had been reported by other women, that he had committed some awful crime and they were looking for any clues as to his whereabouts, without wanting to frighten the public.

I climbed back into bed and slept for four hours. Maddie came in to wake me, worried I had died or something probably. At this point anything could happen. I laughed it off, dragged myself downstairs and smoked three cigarettes in the garden. My phone went again and I jumped. I took it back upstairs and switched it off, hiding it under my clothes in the top drawer. Creaking back down the stairs, I sat down at the piano, asking my fingers to remember pieces learnt some thirty years ago, which they did, falteringly, giving a new edgy tempo and random speedings up and slowings down to a Brahms waltz, a Chopin nocturne, and a piece by Clementi I could only remember half of. Having exhausted my repertoire, I moved into the massage chair. Invisible robot hands pounded up and down my back, and the chair arched and curled me up to a rhythm of its own. As it worked on me I felt tears gather in my eyes and roll down my cheeks, first just one or two, then pouring down until my face was wet. I stared at the ceiling and for a second I was a baby, waiting for someone to come and pick me up and take me away, hold me until I was calm again. As my muscles reluctantly softened, they released tension I didn't know I was holding, leaving me helpless, hopeless, without fight or flight, good for nothing but weeping for everything I had ever lost.

As the chair juddered to a halt I just lay there staring at the ceiling. Maddie came and put it upright again.

"Shall I run you a bath?"

I didn't answer, so she did it anyway. I sank under the hot water, watching an unfamiliar ceiling go wishy washy before my eyes, let out a breath and surged to the surface, causing a tidal wave that narrowly missed my pile of towels on the floor. I lay in the stillness and silence thinking nothing at all, then heaved my heavy body out and pulled the plug out, watching the water drain away, unwanted, dragged back into the ground from where it had come.

I took the phone out of the drawer. As I did so, a message flashed up.

I know where you are. You can't hide from me anymore.

I lay in silence on my bed, feeling my hair wet on the pillow, remembering how they used to say you'd get a cold like that. I was paralysed, unable to make the decision to go. Stepping out of the trench and racing through no-man's land wasn't an option. I slept some more, still wrapped in my towel, pulling the duvet round me on each side. I woke at one and went to the bathroom, feeling the weight of my limbs with every step. I looked at my reflection in the mirror and puffy frightened eyes stared back, questioning, what now?

• •

CHAPTER 25

Sunday

I left as the sun was rising. It must have been before six. I think I was surprised to have woken up alive. Maddie was a late riser and we had said our goodbyes at midnight. I texted her to make sure she locked the doors and kept to the back of the house, just in case

I was half way back to London, a few miles from where Sally lived with her no-good boyfriend when I ran into stationery traffic and sent her a message. Could I pop in? He wouldn't find me there. Her reply to my text arrived within seconds.

I'm here. Come over.

Ensconced in the most comfortable armchair in the world, I fumbled through the story nursing a cup of tea. Sally nodded, frowned, gasped, sighed and listened until I got to the end. But it wasn't the end. I was still waiting for that to happen.

"Am I going mad?"

"You're not going mad Rach, but he is messing with your head, and you need some, what do Americans call it? Closure?"

"I don't think it's just for Americans, but yes. I need answers. I want to know why, what was the endgame?"

"Possibly nothing at all. Just like you said to me about Graham. If he is a psychopath, there is probably no endgame at all. It's just a process he goes through, where everything he does is completely alien to us, but we reframe it to make it fit, because basically we have no concept of someone behaving like this. It's too hard to comprehend. We rationalise, tell it as we want it to be rather than like it is."

"And what about you? What news of Mr Commitment? Still on the scene?"

Sally ran her hand through her unkempt hair and stared out of the window before turning back with a sad face. "He goes home two nights a week now. When he's here, it's a bit tense, and he won't go out with me anywhere."

"What happened to funny?"

"It's in there somewhere, I know it is. I know there is a lovely man who's just frightened to be himself."

"You're sure he's lovely? Did you ever check him out?"

"In what way?"

"Well, do you know for sure he was on oil rigs?"

Sally stared at me, then out of the window. "No, I guess I don't."

We sat in the silence that only friends can share. Then she said "He says he's going to change things, make things different for us."

"You and Maddie both."

"Oh?"

"Chris says that to her, you know, that eventually they will be together but just not yet. He doesn't want to upset the kids just before GCSEs and stuff."

"It makes you wonder what's worse, knowing about the wife, or them pretending they haven't got one."

"Like Harry."

"Oh Sal, what do you think this is all about?"

CHAPTER 26

Either you do or you don't

The answer came in the empty days that followed. No reply from Belinda about whether Harry had booked Highfield Manor for August, nothing from the FA, and not a word from Harry. Day after day I watched his WhatsApp photo and status change, from scenes of the City of London after the Borough Market incident, to moody selfies in designer shades that screamed "watch out". Back in New Malden, I got into the habit of putting a chain on the door, not just at night. I told the children it was a new rule and it invalidated the insurance if we didn't do it.

"When did you start caring about rules Mummy?" was the response.

Messages came in from Jess, and she accepted my version of events with a sadness that made me feel I had failed. *"He is still a good man, he has a good heart,"* she said, *"His feelings were real."* I must be a bad, bad person not to have appreciated that. Now it was too late. I messaged Maya and

Caro with an update and they came back straight-away, with concerns about my safety, my well-being, my mental state, and I assured them I was *fine.* Anything less would have paved the way for *I told you so*. The truth was that I was numb. I felt nothing but emptiness.

The last person I told was Isabel. She hadn't come to my party, and I hadn't seen her since that dinner on the first night Harry cancelled our date. From time to time she had crossed my mind. When I was lying in Harry's arms, safe from the world. I wanted to tell her things had turned out okay. But now I was glad I never had. I sent her a message just telling her she had been right about him all along. She sent me a smiley face and some kisses.

I began to sink into a dark place somewhere between sickness and sadness, sleeping all day, lying awake all night. I told Sadie and Josh with enforced cheerfulness that I'd had a change of heart, that I'd decided Harry wasn't the one for me after all. They didn't react with any memorable joy, surprise or disbelief, just took it in their stride, the way they had learnt to since the day their safe world had been rocked all those years ago by their father's breakdown, our divorce and the house move. I told them we were on good terms, that there were no hard feelings. I realise that was a mistake now, because of what happened to Josh, but it seemed a good idea at the time.

It was a week after I got home that I finally went to the police station as instructed. The reception area was stuffy and smelt of damp. I took my place in the queue while men in boiler suits walked through carrying drills, waving their passes at the sergeant on duty. In front of me, a girl in a pink fur jacket with a baby in a pram was brushing tears from her eyes, looking around anxiously, and then up at the clock on the wall. In front of her, a stocky bald man cleared his throat, one elbow on the counter, and spoke loudly through the glass. He was taken through the alarmed door by the desk officer. I wondered what he'd done, or what someone thought he'd done. Perhaps he was innocent, just in the wrong place at the wrong time, a victim of someone else's paranoia or mistaken identity, and was already plotting his revenge on his accuser.

The pink woman was next. I couldn't hear what she said because the drilling had started somewhere at the back of the building. They moved her to the side where she filled in some forms, rocking the pram expertly with her left foot.

Then it was my turn. I told the tired face in front of me that I'd been asked to come down to talk about a crime. As I spoke, I heard myself apologising, felt the heat of embarrassment rise up through me, because suddenly I didn't know why I was there, what Harry had done, or even whether it was in fact me who was guilty. Distrust and paranoia had brought me here. I was a fake, an imposter, an attention seeker.

There was a nod, a buzz on a pager and two officers appeared, one holding open the security barrier while the other ushered me through. We walked down narrow carpeted corridors to a small hot room with no windows. I sat opposite them on a plastic chair, feeling suddenly like a fraud, wasting police time.

One officer asked the questions while the other wrote furiously on a notepad, occasionally asking me to repeat things, sign things, explain things. There was nothing to look at apart from their blank faces, asking why I wouldn't let them take on this man, come down on him like a ton of bricks for something I couldn't even prove.

"When was the last time you heard from him?"

"Last week, sometime. He said he was coming for me."

It sounded pathetic, repeating the words like that. I almost saw the younger officer smirk.

"And have you told him you no longer wish him to contact you?" asked the female officer.

I hesitated. "No. Not in so many words. I suppose it's all been about keeping the volume down, placating him."

The officers exchanged glances.

“Is that what you want? You want him to stop all contact with you?”

“I suppose so.”

The female officer smiled a patronising smile and looked at her watch. “Well either you do, or you don’t. We can’t move forward with this until you make that clear.”

Tears rose in my eyes. "I wished... I mean... He frightens me. He’s lied to me. I want to know what the truth is. I don’t want him to do this to someone else. I want to feel safe.” I was sounding stark raving mad. I could see it on their faces, but she carried on reciting her script.

“We take abusive relationships very seriously indeed. Especially where there are children involved, obviously.”

“And apparently he has a criminal record for causing death by drunk driving.”

They said nothing, just looked at each other. The younger one raised his eyebrows.

“Well does he?” I stared at him, wondering if I could break him if I stared hard enough. At least he was the first to look away.

“We can’t disclose details like that I’m afraid.”

“Or whether there was a laptop stolen at Godalming station? Because if that’s not true then yes he has extorted money from me, and it’s a crime and yes I want to report it."

"That is a matter for the transport police, so it's up to their procedures I'm afraid how much information they can divulge."

"What about the FA? Can't you find out if he was lying about that?"

"They have their own confidentiality procedures which we can't interfere with without a good reason."

All roads led to nothing. Now, as in all my darkest moments a voice in my head berated me for throwing away this relationship, this man who loved me more than the world, because of my paranoid delusions. I was nothing more than a fantasist.

I let myself go a bit after that. The words poured out like vomit. I said I was worried that it was all a hoax, that it was making me crazy not knowing what was true or not. I didn't trust my own judgment anymore. If there was all that cash flying around, why would he be pursuing me for the odd fifty quid? The shell companies owned by Harry, his father and Mark Rathbone had all been set up by the same outfit. But that could mean nothing just as much as everything.

They didn't react to any of this, just took more notes, nodded, and when I'd finished, glanced at each other and shuffled their papers in symmetrical unison, like images in a mirror.

"I'm going to ask you one more time, because it is important we are absolutely clear on this. Would you like us to track this man down and have a word with him?"

My heart was already racing at the thought of it.

"No. Please don't do that. If you go looking for him he will see you coming, he'll know I've sent you and he'll come for me. I just want to find out why he lied. And I want not to be scared anymore. I want you to tell me that I don't need to be afraid, which means I need to know the truth." I was ranting like a mad woman.

"I understand", said the female officer, whose job it was to tame me, make me compliant, use her sisterhood act to get me to give them the green light. "This happens, and it isn't your fault. You were blindsided, and you mustn't give yourself a hard time for something you had no control over."

"I'm not giving myself a hard time. You are."

The officers raised eyebrows at each other before the woman carried on. "I'm sorry but like I say, our hands are tied. Either you authorise us to pay him a visit or you don't. If you don't, then nothing more will happen. It's up to you."

I said nothing, just hung my head, hating this.

"You don't want to take it any further? Are

you absolutely sure?"

I nodded, and they stood up in unison, scraping their chairs, choreographing my exit.

"Well don't hesitate to get in touch if there is anything else, or if you change your mind. Someone from CID will give you a call in a few days' time."

It was the longest weekend. My first one without either Harry or the kids to keep me company. To keep myself busy I fired off various messages to other people, about work, exams, holiday plans, a yoga class.

I kept my phone beside me all weekend, just in case. Just in case of what – I wasn't sure. Deep down I probably wanted someone to call and say there had been some terrible mistake, that the glitch had been fixed and that the universe would be operating normally again from now on. Even a call from CID would have done, a friendly voice asking if I was okay, whether I'd had second thoughts. Then I found myself texting Julie.

Just checking in to see if you've seen our friend at all since we spoke.

Her reply came back a few minutes later

Not seen him. Are you okay?

Yes, I'm okay. Still can't piece it all together though.

Well, like I said, I think keep away from that man, if you can.

Thanks Julie. Will do. Take care x

Her words *if you can* stuck with me. I checked and double checked the chain on the door that night.

Then Maya called. It was Sunday afternoon and the children were with Adam for lunch. I was lying on the sofa in the dark, heavy curtains shutting out the June sunshine. I was dragged from deep sleep by the ringtone which took a while to register. For a second I thought it was my alarm and it was Monday morning. I fumbled for the phone and managed a hoarse *hello.*

"Rach, it's me. Is everything okay?"

"Yes, sort of. What do you mean?"

"I mean, are you okay, right now? Where are you?"

"At home. Been asleep. What's up?"

"I mean, well this is going to sound weird, but have you heard from Harry at all?"

"Not for a while. Why?"

"I think I just saw him."

"Where?" My heart leapt and pounded, stomach churned.

"Look, I'm not a hundred percent sure it was him."

"Where?"

"Going into Maddie's house."

I sank back down into the sofa, my heartbeat loud in my chest, blood pumping in my ears. I felt sick. "When?"

"About ten minutes ago. I recognised him first by the way he walks, you know that kind of swagger he has. He didn't look like himself in any other way actually. He was wearing shades and a baseball cap. He was on his phone, jacket slung over one shoulder, then he got to her house and rang the bell."

"She let him in? You saw her let him in?" Fury and fear filled my body as I waited for her response.

"Well yes, I mean I presume she did, because the next minute he was inside with the door shut."

"What do you think it is? What's going on? Has she been seeing him all along?"

"Look, I feel bad for telling you all this, especially as we have no idea about the circumstances. It may be completely innocent. He may have come to pick up his stuff. Who knows?"

"She would have told me if she was going to see him again. And she wouldn't be seeing him again, not after everything we went through. It doesn't make sense."

"When did you last hear from her?"

"A few days ago? I don't know. Not since Devon. She's been quiet for a while I suppose. Quieter than usual."

"Well I didn't know what to do. I didn't

know whether to say... I hope I've done the right thing telling you."

"Yes, you've done the right thing."

"Good. I hope so."

"Let me have a think. I need to think." My brain was refusing to get into gear. I said goodbye and closed my eyes, concentrating as hard as I could. Maddie, who had said we were okay, that the past was water under the bridge, was getting her revenge at last. I took deep breaths, knowing that anger was not the answer, and that anything I decided to do right now wouldn't be the right decision.

I called Jess and told her.

"Can you talk to Maddie, find out what's going on?" she suggested, predictably.

"I don't know if I even want to know."

"And do you know for sure it was him?"

"Maya says she recognised his swagger."

"Ah, I remember that. It was kinda unique."

"What do you think?"

"I think you call Maddie. There is probably a perfectly reasonable explanation for it all. And it probably wasn't even him. Don't catastrophise Rach, it isn't worth panicking before there's good reason to. If you don't call her, you will sit and assume it's what you think. If you do call her, there's a chance of a decent explanation."

I didn't want to even take the risk of having my worst imaginings confirmed. Instead of calling I sent her a message on WhatsApp asking for a chat.

Sorry Rach, I'm working all day but will give you a call tonight – all okay with you?

I didn't reply.

Because a few hours later I got a call from Sam Dawson.

CHAPTER 27

Any other name

"I'm sorry to bother you. Is that Rachel?"

"It is. Who's this?"

"I'm Samantha Brize-Dawson."

The split second that followed before I replied spun out like an eternity before me, as images from the last weeks slapped down on top of each other like centuries of wallpaper. Guildford, horse jumps, sand dunes, ornaments on a windowsill, images of motorbikes, hands patting empty pockets.

"Sam? Sorry, you mean... as in Harry?"

"Harry?" She was confused. Then I remembered.

"I mean as in Jonathan. Jonathan Dawson, sorry – you're Sam Dawson as in Jonathan..." I was tripping over my words, my eyes seemed to blur with confusion. She sounded young, kind, shy, out of her depth already, and now so was I.

"Yes, as in Jonathan, I suppose, yes." She

seemed hesitant. There was a brief pause as I tried to compose myself.

"So, how...?" I hesitated, not sure if this was really happening.

"Julie gave me your number."

"Julie?" All I could do was repeat names, it seemed. She must think I was some kind of space cadet.

"Jo's neighbour Julie. She said you had been back in touch and that maybe it would be good if I gave you a call."

"Ah, okay, I'm glad you did. I have so many questions, so much has happened I don't know where to begin."

"I think I may be able to help straighten a few things out. Can we meet?"

I looked at my watch. "Today?"

"Today, if you can."

"I can. Where?"

"I know this sounds odd, but there's a car park just off the Chertsey Road, near the M25. I'll send you the postcode. How soon do you think you can be there?"

"In an hour, tops."

The phone buzzed again straightaway with the postcode and I copied it into Google Maps. It would mean leaving now, and that meant I'd miss collecting Josh at the station at the usual time. I texted him to say I'd had to go out in an emergency and that I'd ask Maya or someone if they could drop him home. He sent me a thumbs up. I climbed into the car and started the engine.

The traffic was frustratingly slow on Burlington Road, then on the A3 it slowed to a standstill. I pulled into a petrol station to go online. Maya was asking how I was, what I wanted to do about the Maddie situation. Her second message must have come after I didn't answer for a few minutes, because by then she had looked me up on the app and seen me heading for the depths of Surrey.

Where the hell are you?

There wasn't time to text. Then, pulling out of the garage, I remembered I hadn't actually asked her to collect Josh, but had just used the Dorset WhatsApp group to post a general request.

Anyone free to collect Josh from station at 4.30 and drop him home? I'm just pursuing a lead.

Then, realising that wasn't enough.

I think I've found his wife.

The Chertsey Road is like any other road in Surrey. Nondescript, suburban semis give way to recreation grounds, then areas of woodland. It was between the woods and a children's playground that I found the car park, a good twenty minutes before I should have been there. Sam might come early as well. She seemed in a hurry to see me and we hadn't fixed an exact time. I reversed into a space at the far end of the car park, then changed my mind and turned the car round, suddenly thinking I'd like to see her before she saw me, somehow get the upper hand by spotting her in the mirror first.

My heart was pumping hard. I only noticed when I switched off the engine. The noise was almost the same level. I picked up my phone but my hands were sweating too much to operate the touch screen. Taking a few deep breaths, I told myself everything was okay, that this last mission was all I needed to put the finishing pieces of the jigsaw in place. I opened WhatsApp first. Maya had replied that she couldn't do the pick-up but that she could ask Simon as he was home early from work, and good luck with the mysterious mission. Maddie had opened the message but not replied.

I was just opening Snapchat as a further distraction from my nerves, when a car pulled in next to me. I hadn't seen it coming, despite the mirror plan, and now I was looking through my passenger window straight at the face that belonged to a voice I had heard for the first time only an hour earlier. It belonged to a diminutive slip of a girl in her mid-twenties. So this was her. This was Sam Brize. Not the man Harry Dawson set up his business with, and probably not his wife either. For a second, I was too shocked to move. Slowly and almost gracefully, she opened her door, stepped out of the car and motioned as if to ask if she could get into mine. I nodded, moving my mess off the seat and dusting off the crumbs that seemed to permanently nestle in the stitching lines. The door opened in slow motion, and the noise of the traffic hit me for a brief second until she shut it behind her. We looked at each other. For some reason I wanted to cry.

"Thanks for coming," I said.

"Shall we drive?" she replied. "I'd feel safer if we were moving."

"If you want," I said. "What do you mean, safer?"

She looked over her shoulder, the way I had done so often since meeting the man who had overturned my world, and back at me.

"I suppose we're okay here for a bit, but it's not good that we're meeting. He won't like it."

"I see, okay, let's do that." I put the key in the ignition and switched on the engine. "Do you have anywhere in mind?"

"I can direct you to somewhere a bit more off the beaten track."

"Okay, can I just check something first? I need to see if my son got home okay."

"Sure."

I opened up WhatsApp again, and there was still no answer from Maddie, and no message anywhere from Simon. I rang Josh, but it went to voicemail. "Shit, where is he?"

"Do you have find my friends? Share my location?" suggested Sam. "Where's he supposed to be?"

"A friend is supposed to be collecting him from the station. I have that thing on Snapchat, unless he's gone into, what do you call it?"

"Ghost mode?"

"That's it. How are you so savvy about it then?"

"It's a bit old hat to be honest, but it was fun a few years ago. Everyone used it."

"I don't remember that."

"I'm only twenty-five remember. It's what we live on, Snapchat, Instagram."

"Twenty-five?"

I opened SnapMaps to see a screen crowded with avatars. I saw Sadie still at school, probably rehearsing the musical again, and Maya at the office, Jess at the café, and Maddie… I squinted at the screen, zoomed in some more, Maddie on the M25, and another avatar just next to her, almost on top of hers. It was Josh.

"Oh my God. I don't believe it."

"What? Is everything okay?"

"I don't know. Something weird is happening. Take a look at this."

Sam leaned over the phone, pulling her long

hair over to the other side as she did so. She smelt of bubble bath.

"Who are these two?"

"That's my friend Maddie, and that's Josh, my son."

"So that's okay then, she's picked him up."

"Yes, but it wasn't supposed to be her, and why is she coming down the A3 with him?"

"They're coming here? Why?"

"I don't know. Not sure why they would, unless they're following me, because she's worried about me?"

Sam's face changed. "Do they know something? Do you trust her?"

"Of course." I said it without thinking. Sam must have seen my face change, but didn't say anything. I couldn't go there now. "It just doesn't make any sense. Do you think this app always tells the truth? I mean, are they definitely there, exactly there where it says?"

"Yeah, well at least their phones are there, but you can't have a car without a person, and how old did you say Josh was?"

"Fifteen, just."

"So it can't be him driving."

I collected my thoughts. If you can't solve a problem, think about something else, then when you come back to it, things sometimes fall into place. I looked at Sam, who looked back at me, wide-eyed, questioning.

"You said you were twenty-five." I said, half to myself.

"Yes, why? Dad, Jonathan, was only eighteen when he had me."

I turned towards her. "Say that again?"

"Dad, well it feels weird calling him that, after everything that happened. But I guess that's what he is, technically, even though we hardly speak anymore. He sends money, wants me to succeed, set up a business, even set one up for me, with me on the paperwork, said I could do what I liked and he'd support me. I wanted to run a mobile beauty business."

That made sense. I stared ahead at the row of conifers in front of the car, sentries standing to attention, blocking my way, holding me hostage. They were the end of the road, the blind alley.

"I feel such an idiot. I didn't realise..."

"You thought I was his wife, didn't you?"

"I did."

"I guessed that. Didn't want to tell you everything on the phone. I wanted to see who you were, because Julie said – well she said he wasn't being straight with you, and you sounded like you needed to know."

I switched the engine off again. "No, he wasn't straight with me. I mean, he said he had three children, but it was a lot of other lies, about what he did for a living, about cars, motorbikes, watches, millions of pounds…."

"How many children?"

"Three."

She nodded, turned away, then back to me.

"He did have three."

"Did have?"

"My brother died."

"God, Sam, I am so, so sorry."

"He was fifteen, I was seventeen, when it happened."

"What happened?"

They divorced when I was three. Mum hated Dad seeing us because of the drugs. He was high on coke the whole time. Cheated on her when she was pregnant with some junkie called Nicky."

The sickness rose in my stomach again. Sam went on, talking more quickly, in bursts, turning every so often to look behind us.

"She only let him visit once a month, and only in her house, the one at Blakeley Avenue where Gran lives now. She'd leave him in the sitting room for two hours with us. Never let him take us anywhere."

"Must have been awful, for all of you," I said, in what turned out to be a whisper.

"Pretty awful. I mean, at the time, I thought

Mum was so mean to Dad, I thought he was the handsome prince and she was an evil witch, but that's probably how he put it."

"He didn't hurt you, did he?"

"No abuse, nothing like that. Not that I remember, and I'm sure Mum wouldn't have let it happen. She was in the next room. The door was open. It was just, well, stressful."

"I can imagine." I glanced at the phone again. Maddie's car was stuck in traffic somewhere on the M25, probably a good fifteen minutes away, but it was still bothering me that Josh was with her. "So how did the accident happen?"

"We were getting older, more bolshy I suppose. I was about to turn eighteen. Dad said he wanted to take me out for my birthday. Mum said no way. But he turned up, drunk, high, and with Nicky in the car. He told us to get in. We were scared. Mum tried to stop him, but he hit her."

"Hit her?"

"I'd never seen him hit anyone before. But he hit her and she collapsed on the doorstep and he yelled at us to get in the car. We were scared, so we got in, and he just revved the engine and pulled out of the drive, turning right just as a car was coming from the right, and another one overtaking in the other lane. At least that's what they told us afterwards. It was a head on collision. Dad and Nicky were saved by the airbag, and I had put my seatbelt on, so we were all okay, even the driver of the other car survived, but not ….." Sam put her head in her hands

"Oh my God." I pictured the driveway to the house, the traffic racing down Blakeley Avenue. I had stood in that spot.

"I'm so sorry, I don't know what to say."

"You don't need to say anything." An ambulance raced past on the main road, as if to illustrate the story.

"Your brother died at the scene?"

"He flew forwards, crashing into Dad. Died instantly."

"Do you….. do you remember… anything?"

"Nothing. It's a blank. They said I lost consciousness."

Tears were in her eyes now. I was shaking. I put my hands on the wheel to steady them, then back in my lap. I stared at the sentinel trees.

"I can't imagine how awful that must have been."

"I don't talk about it much. I'm sorry." She wiped her eyes on her sleeve.

"You have nothing to be sorry for."

Sam wiped her eyes on her sleeve and sat upright, pointing at the phone. "Where's your friend?"

We looked at the app again. The avatars were moving slowly further towards mine. With trembling hands now, I dialled Josh's number again, but it went to voicemail. Then I dialled Maddie. It rang once, then went to voicemail. *Decline call* I thought. Then *Why would she do that?* It must be fear of getting stopped by the police. Maddie's car was a tiny primitive thing, fitted barely more than a couple of miniature adults and a handbag. She wouldn't have a hands-free phone – it just wasn't her. I put the phone on my lap, turned back to Sam. There was still so much I didn't know.

"You said there were three children, I mean, before your brother died."

"There was a baby in the car. With Dad and Nicky."

"*Their* baby?"

"Yes."

"Did you know about it, at the time, I mean?"

"No. We got in the car. I think we both thought it was her baby. Wouldn't have dawned on us it was our half-brother. That was the thing, you see…" she broke off,

"What do you mean?"

"My brother died because the baby seat was in the car. He couldn't find the seatbelt for the middle seat at the back. There probably wasn't one. Dad didn't wait. Mum was coming out of the house, screaming at him to stop, and he didn't. He just slammed his foot down and pulled out of the drive, turning right into the traffic."

"Jesus."

We sat in silence for a few moments.

"Where is he now – the baby?"

"With Nicky, I mean, maybe with Dad and Nicky, I guess, now he's out of prison."

I let it all sink in, as far as it could. Sometimes people tell you so much that you can't absorb it, like watering a parched plant.

In my mind, I saw Isabel Taylor's face, looking at his Tinder photo and straight back at me, turning the phone back towards me on the table.

"Prison. How long?"

"Eight years."

He had only been out a few months when we met.

"So, what about Julie?"

"Oh Julie knows everything, but she feels conflicted or something."

"In what way?"

"She likes Gran, doesn't want the world to know about Dad, to protect Gran from all the gossip, so she keeps things on the down low."

"She said they barely knew each other. Now I get why. That's good of her, I suppose."

"And I have cried on her shoulder a few times, when it seemed like there wasn't anyone else, you know."

"What about your mother?"

She seemed not to even breathe for a few seconds, then turned to me, breathed slowly, the longest, slowest breath in and then out again. "She killed herself."

What happened in our minds for the next few minutes I don't know. Mine was a mess. Sam was very still. Cars hummed, oblivious, down the dual carriageway in front of us. A plane roared overhead, soaring skywards to a better place. From its tiny windows, we were invisible dots on a patchwork landscape. Clouds were gathering overhead, racing across the sky as the wind picked up, whipping the branches of the trees in front of us and a flurry of raindrops thrashed the windscreen. Nature was urging us on, like a Grand National spectator pounding their horse to victory from the sofa. But nature had no say anymore. It was down to human intervention.

"What do you want to do?"

"I don't know." I didn't know. And when I didn't know what to do, I'd usually ask Maya, or Jess. I phoned Maya.

"Rach, I was just about to call you."

"What's happened?"

"Josh was a no-show at the station."

"That's because he's with Maddie. It seems she picked him up and is on her way here.

"That's the other thing. It can't be her. She's in hospital."

"But the app says she's half way round the M25, following me."

"Well it's not her then. She's been quite badly beaten up. The ambulance arrived. I only knew because Simon was putting the rubbish out, and that's weird enough for a start, but he saw them taking her out of the house on a stretcher. He offered to go with them but her boyfriend, that Chris guy, had turned up. She wasn't answering her phone. He was all over the place. He's with her in hospital now I think."

"So who's got her car, and her phone?"

There was silence. I heard my heart beating, the blood pumping in my ears.

"Oh my God Maya, it's not just her car and her phone he's got."

"What do you mean? Who do you mean? Oh my God, not Harry?"

"He's got Josh."

Sam had one hand on the door as she listened, wide-eyed to our conversation.

"He's coming isn't he?"

Maya heard her voice. "Who are you with? His wife?"

"I'm with Sam, his daughter. But I think we need to get going."

I hung up and started the engine, tears rolling down my face now. Sam took over the logical role and reached across me to turn it back off.

“Don’t drive yet,” she said."Make a plan."

“I have to make sure Josh is okay.”

She took my phone, opened Snapchat again.

“We need to put it on ghost mode. That’s how he knows where we are.”

“But I want to find Josh,” I said, taking the phone back. “If you do that, I can’t see him. And I want him to find me because I want him to be here. With me.”

“Okay. Let’s think.”

“We haven’t got time to think,” I said, trying to breathe but only finding breaths that came in panicky bursts.

“Get in my car. Switch off your lock screen so the app stays open, and get in my car. That way he comes here, but we won’t be here. We can be over there." She indicated a dirt track concealed by a concrete building.

I obeyed, with no other option. Before we left, Sam screenshotted the numbers for Josh and Maddie, then was scrolling through my contacts for another one.

“Which Jonathan is it? There are three of them.”

“It’s not Jonathan. It’s Harry.”

"What?" She stopped for a second and stared at me.

"He calls himself Harry?"

"I know, it's some sort of nickname or middle name. He told me his real name was Jonathan."

"He calls himself Harry" she repeated. "Harry wasn't any of his names."

"What?" I absorbed what she was saying before she said it.

"Harry was my brother."

I was silent as that sank in. Sam looked at me.

"He could have had any other name." The sky was dark now, headlights were going on, and big fat droplets of rain were hitting the windscreen, faster, harder. "But he took Harry's."

"I'm so sorry Sam. All I can say is none of this is your fault. What he has done, the way he has lived his life, none of it is your responsibility."

"He was my little brother."

"I know." I reached out and held her hand. "Come on, we can do this."

I took the phone off her, found the number and let her photograph it. Then I scrambled out of my side and ran around to her door, took her by the arm, pulled her out.

"Come on, let's do it. Don't give up."

We made a dash through the rain and climbed into her car. It smelt of bubble bath and handcream. I fastened my seatbelt and we reversed out of the car park, bumped down the track and came to a halt behind the building.

"What now?" she asked, white as sheet, staring ahead at the rush hour traffic moving slowly along the main road. My car, which Harry knew well enough, would be visible from a hundred metres away, but Sam's Mini could only be seen from the far end of the car park, and even then only partly. From inside the car, we had a decent view of anyone indicating left to come off the road, although there was obviously no guarantee that Harry would be in the mood to obey the highway code.

"We need to phone 999. They can intercept him." I said. "Can you do that?"

"Yes, yes, of course." She reached into her pocket for her phone, pressed the home button, shook it, pressed the button again, then turned and looked at me, horror-struck.

"What is it?"

"The battery's just died" she said.

"Shit, we'll have to go back to the car for mine."

"You can't do that. He'll see you." Her voice was raised in a panic now. "Rachel, please. He will be here any minute. And it defeats the object. If the phone is with us, he finds us first."

"I'll turn off the app. It'll be fine."

"There's no time to get back there, even if you run."

I bit my lip, my hand on the door handle, unsure. She was in no state to make a decision. I was twice her age, and probably twice her size, which meant nothing in reality but in the heat of the moment, anthropologically maybe, it mattered.

"What choice do I have? The police are my only hope. Your father has kidnapped my son." I was opening the car door before I'd finished the sentence and slammed it hard, shutting out Sam's pleading voice and ghostly face. The wind whipped my hair into my face and the rain came down harder. The noise of the road was more deafening from here, and my heart thumped in panicky rhythm, disabling me, making me slow, clumsy. I raced down the dirt track and back through the sentinel trees into the car park, clicking frantically on the unlock button until the orange lights flashed in response. Opening the driver's door, I reached inside, scanning the seats for the phone, while feeling the door close hard against my calves. I spotted the phone just between the two front seats and made a grab for it, but just as my fingers closed around it, another hand was on mine, squeezing my fingers so I screamed and let go, and then the door slammed on my calves again, making me cry out in pain.

"I don't think you'll be needing that." Stars of pain swam before my eyes. I must have fallen head-first onto the handbrake because I blacked out for a second. Then the world righted itself and I struggled backwards, stood up and steadied myself, looking around for Maddie's car. It was a few metres away from me, driver and passenger door open, both seats empty. No Harry, No Josh. No Sam.

"Josh!" I yelled, louder than I have ever screamed in my life. "Josh!"

I have found myself without my phone plenty of times, leaving it at home, taking it in for repairs, or just not being able to find it for a few desperate minutes, and every time it has felt like the end of the world. "Can you phone my phone!" I have shouted at nobody in particular, then raced out to listen in the car, in the bathroom, in the fridge. A few seconds separation from a device that I spent the first half of my life without can lead me to paroxysms of anxiety that will be familiar to most of the population of the western world. But right then, as I stared wildly around that deserted gravel car park while the oblivious world roared past, those moments were thrown into a void of insignificance.

I screamed Josh's name again, then Sam's, then Harry's, then *Help* until my voice was hoarse. The rain pounded into puddles. I heard nothing back but the hum of lorries. Holding my hair out of my face I raced towards the trees, back to Sam's car. The driver door was open. It was empty. My skin prickled with fear as I walked around it, stopping at the garage that had been our shelter from the enemy, or should have been, if I hadn't abandoned it on a hapless mission. It was a plain, rectangular brick structure of no apparent purpose, a storage facility of some sort, or the housing for some sort of machinery. It didn't matter. Paint was peeling off the wooden door which stood, creaking open and banging shut as the wind gusted. I opened it, truly and honestly expecting death.

In the darkness, a small voice whispered "Mum? Is that you?"

Without a phone torch to help, I fumbled in the darkness for longer than I should have with the ropes around his wrists and ankles. But when he was free, I held him closer than I have ever held anyone, and had the most extraordinary feeling inside, as if fire was burning in my stomach, a feeling I would now describe as a mixture of relief and wild, wild rage.

"Can you walk? Do you think you can run?" I don't know why I asked him that. It was as if I was doing a quick survey of our stock, an inventory of our arsenal which would help me make the next decision.

"I think so. Where are we going?"

"Did he hurt you?"

"No, not really."

"What did he say to you?"

"That you were in trouble, that he needed to help sort it out and that he wanted me to help. As back up or something."

"Back up?"

"To be honest, I didn't think much about it. He said you were in trouble. That he had to stop you getting hurt by someone very dangerous."

"Sorry Josh, of course, I understand completely." I found myself stroking his hair, wiping the tears from his face, while mine flowed undeterred.

"Then he made me find you."

"He what? How?"

"On the app of course. That's how we knew where you were. But I figured that if we used my phone then you'd see where I was."

I hugged him tighter. "You are a genius. He is an idiot, and he thinks he works in tech. What did he say when he brought you in here, tied you up?"

"He said I had to stay very quiet because it wasn't safe. He said I mustn't move, mustn't make a sound or something really bad could happen. I wasn't scared that he'd actually do anything to me, but he was just behaving really weirdly. Like a kind of robot or something."

I wiped my wet face with my sleeve. "Josh, I have no idea. Something must be going on in his head, but the important thing is that you're okay.

"What do we do now?"

All I wanted to do was get home.

"Can we go home, Mum?"

"Yes, we can go home, but the girl I came to meet here, Harry's daughter, as it turns out, this is her car." I ushered him out of the door and pointed.

"She's gone," he said.

"She's gone."

"Do you think he took her with him?"

"I don't know Josh, Can you think back for me. Did he say anything at all about his children?"

"He was ranting on about stuff all the way down here. To start with he was saying what a great boy I was, how lucky you were to have me, how he remembered when his son was my age, stuff like that."

"Did he say his son's name"

"Not sure. He mentioned Sam."

"Sam. That's his daughter. That's who I came to see."

"Why did you want to see her?"

"To find things out, but it doesn't matter now. I need to find her, Josh. Can you come with me? I need to see if she's okay."

"Sure, let's try this way."

The dirt track led to what looked like a

gravel pit, half dug, half filled in with rubble, scrap metal, sheets of plastic and plywood. Tyre tracks had worn a path to the left, now a mud bath, which led to some more garages, not dissimilar to the one by the car park but more run down, with corrugated iron roofs and broken windows. I glanced into the pit at the rubble, then down towards the ramshackle buildings beyond.

"Are you going to call her, see if she's hiding somewhere?"

"I don't want to shout, in case *he*'s still here."

"We can do an army manoeuvre if you like, where you cover me as I go forward, and then..."

"No, Josh, we're not doing that."

And we stood there in the rain for a second, before I looked, and had to blink a few times to check I wasn't imagining it. I could see a hand amongst the rubble. The plywood was moving, and Sam's tiny figure slid out from underneath. The relief was enormous.

"I could hear you. Thanks for not shouting though. I think he may be somewhere around."

"How did you get away?"

"I ran as soon as I saw the car pull in. Sorry, not very sisterhood of me, but it was like autopilot. I crawled in here. He came lumbering past, but must have carried on that way."

"Did he know it was you? In the car?" I gave her a hand up the last bit of the slope and she dusted herself off.

"I don't know. I don't know what he knows. He didn't call my name, I just heard his breathing, his footsteps, his .... Sobbing – I think." She was crying too now, or maybe it was the rain on her face, or the rain that fell between our faces and made the world look sad. I hugged Sam Dawson then, not a family hug or a friend hug, but a hug with no name, a hug that was part sisterhood, part shared tragedy, part unspoken understanding of something impossible to articulate.

"I think he's gone off again."

"Again?"

"He used to disappear, sometimes for months. Mum said it was to get drugs. Then he'd turn up out of the blue from nowhere, as if nothing had happened. Growing up we thought it was normal, having a dad who wasn't there half the time."

Josh was intrigued by her. I imagined him comparing hard luck stories, realising he had come off lightly in our comparatively amicable broken family. But then who knows what children actually feel? Difficult emotions get boxed up and buried before anyone thinks to ask about them, buildings erected on top to prevent accidental discovery, and it's only the therapeutic wrecking ball that can even begin to get close to the truth, dusty and unrecognisable when it emerges to a chorus of *We should have let sleeping dogs lie...*

Harry had gone, and so had my car. We

stood in the rain, waiting for each other to call it – *time of escape 5.14pm* - until Josh spoke up.

"My phone might still be in the little car."

We found it in the driver's door. My fingers hovered over the number 9.

"Are you going to call the police?" Sam asked, biting her lip.

But they were already answering, and I was already telling them where we were, and who they should be looking for. Shortly afterwards, a car arrived to take us home. Another officer stayed to question Sam. She motioned to me to say she'd call.

"Not yet – he has my phone remember?" I called over my shoulder.

She sent me a thumbs up and climbed into the police car and that was the last I saw of her.

CHAPTER 28

Abinger Hammer

It didn't take them long to find him, but seeing the blue lights in the rear view mirror, Harry had sped off, sending cars skidding out of his way, and had held the chasers at bay for a good twenty miles before a collision with a lorry on a notorious stretch of road near Abinger Hammer sent both vehicles plummeting off the road into oblivion. Two bodies were eventually found in the rubble around the wreckage, too badly burnt to be identified.

The story was in the local press the next day, then disappeared from the minds and memories of almost everyone involved, except for a few of us who will never forget.

Maddie recovered from her injuries soon enough. She was too lively to stay down for long. Maya and I were at her bedside a few days later. The police had first dibs on her, but we made her repeat everything just for us. Chris turned up with flowers and sat with his head in his hands as he was forced to hear it all again.

"He turned up on Sunday, then it was basically hell, from that moment on."

Maya and I listened, unable to process what she told us.

"He told me he'd been round to see Rach, that she was threatening to hurt herself. He wanted me to help him get her out of the house, make her safe."

Maddie and Chris took turns to tell snippets of the story, each of them too traumatised to do more than a couple of sentences at a time, and the truth was hard to hear. Once inside Maddie's house, Harry took her phone, forced her to let him into it with her fingerprint ID and sent messages from it to her employer saying she was sick. I remembered him telling me about how his father used to shut him away, not let him eat until he agreed to work for him on some or other dodgy project. And here he was doing the very same thing. And meanwhile, he was reading my WhatsApp message to the group asking for someone to collect Josh.

"I heard the message ping. It has a special ring tone, so I knew it would be you or Maya, and I could hear him through the door tapping out a reply."

The nurse came in and checked the screens. "Not too much excitement now. She's had quite enough for one day." Maddie closed her eyes, letting Chris take over.

Maddie had somehow managed to overpower him enough to get herself out of the bedroom, but Harry proceeded to use his own brute strength to ensure she wasn't leaving with him. It was lucky she was one of the few of us who still had a landline because she would never have been able to crawl out of the house to alert the emergency services otherwise.

"Well either he didn't think about the landline, or he thought he had actually killed her..." Chris was almost sobbing as he spoke, and I thought how we had misjudged him, how I had so easily assumed that my charming online romance was somehow superior to this unconventional but truly loving relationship.

"Maybe he didn't care," I said under my breath.

Maddie managed a few more words then.

"When he left, his last words were: *Babe, you won't be seeing me for a while. I've got to run a couple of errands, then I'm going round to see Rach, because she needs me.*"

So that was the motivation to break down a solid door with her bare hands. I felt humbled. She smiled weakly and closed her eyes.

"I hadn't realised he had taken the car. I could have got them to catch him earlier, maybe."

"It's okay, ssshhh," I stroked her arm, thinking nothing but how much I felt responsible for all of this.

Maddie was in hospital for two weeks in total but came out almost good as new. Her spark was a little diminished, which made her only about three times as exciting as the average person. It was time for us to get on with our lives.

I tried to find Sam, even went down to her home, only to find a Sold sign outside it. I called Julie, texted her, but there was no answer. Something wasn't right about that, I thought in the night when I couldn't sleep. In my half-awake dreams I had visions of them sitting around with Harry, laughing, cackling like witches. I would get up and go to the bathroom, splash water on my face, turn the pillows over, think about my breathing, but my body stiffened as the images came flooding back. One night, unable to get back to sleep, I made the mistake of switching on my laptop and googling the accident again. It was very brief, the sort of half-baked reporting that reflected the importance of non-descript lives. If they had been mothers or children, it might have been different. Society is strange like that, valuing the young so much more highly than the old.

Chris has left his wife now and moved in with Maddie. Jess and Jason are married with a puppy and Maya is still with Simon, rubbing along as well as can be expected. Caro and James have moved to Dorset and we are all angling for an invitation for old times' sake. Sally's part-time lover disappeared in a puff of smoke one day, leaving her to patrol the internet for a replacement.

They have shown me in their own ways that every relationship is as unique as a fingerprint, that we find or miss our chance at happiness based on a multitude of decisions. Fixating on the missing limb can blind you to what is real, and that way, as they say, madness lies. Endings bring beginnings, and craving a happy-ever-after, we can miss out on another outcome no-one has written about yet. The amputation is a viewpoint, a way of looking at things that can just as easily be turned on its head. On the other side of the coin is freedom.

Isabel is still a great friend, with no recriminations, and not a mention of I told you so. They all look after me more than I expect them to. Anna and Sadie fuss around me all the time. Josh is quieter than he used to be, and looks at me with a sad face sometimes, but then I let him beat me at Scrabble and it cheers him up.

Epilogue

June 2018

I am in the back of a taxi driving down the Kings Road, on my way to a meeting. I don't like leaving the house unless I have to. It's what I know, and the only place I feel safe. Maya and Caro keep on at me to get out and about, join a "proper" dating site, take up cycling, join a choir, but the thought fills me with horror. My mind is awash with doubt, and however much I try to banish it, anxiety follows me around like a puppy.

If there hadn't been roadworks at the World's End, if I hadn't happened to be staring out of the window as the lights turned red, I could have been spared. But it must have been meant to be like this. Jess would say that the universe needed me to know something so that I could move on.

I almost don't recognise him at first. He is unshaven, and a full grey beard has replaced the stubble of his charming Tinder photo. His face is ruddy, from sun or drink or both, or scarred maybe, and his eyes are small. I only see them when he pushes his sunglasses onto his head while he reads his phone. In his other hand he's holding a can of Jack Daniels and coke. His shirt is torn, sleeves rolled up to the elbows revealing a noticeable outbreak of psoriasis on both arms.

Next to him on the bench lies a grey rucksack and a couple of plastic bags filled with things of awkward shapes which protrude at angles. Suddenly he leans forwards and shouts something that sounds like "Nicky!". Several people turn, presumably not because they were all called Nicky, but curious as to where the voice is coming from. Then one of them, it must have been her, hurries towards him, gesticulating wildly in the manner of someone in an altered state, with no concept of personal space or demure Britishness. She's wearing tiny shorts and a crop top, too skimpy for her middle-aged body, although there isn't an ounce of fat on her. Her hair is bleach blonde; her skin weathered. A cigarette hangs from her lips. She takes it out as she bends over him, says something I can't hear, then stands up and feels in her pockets for something, moving out of the space between us. He sees me. Our eyes meet. He blinks, holds my gaze for another second, and then the lights go green.

I am early for the appointment as always, checking the time on my phone at least three times as I wait in the lobby on the fourth floor. It smells of coffee and carpets. I stare out of the window at the traffic below, leaf through a dog-eared magazine but can't take anything in. Then the door opens and Doctor Alexander beckons me in with a smile. I take my seat in the leather armchair and we begin. He asks about my journey because he knows I had to come by taxi. We discussed it last time because I was nervous of going out on my own. He is nodding and it makes me well up with tears because it's too much attention.

Then I tell him what I saw. My words come out jumbled, disordered. I am not making any sense. I can't forget those eyes meeting mine, the dawning of recognition, the fear that surged through my body.

He pushes his chair back from the desk and clasps his hands behind his head.

“That's a very vivid account. I can imagine you were afraid.”"

"He's dead. I know he's dead. That wasn't real." I look up, needing him to give me certainty.

Dr Alexander nods slowly, but he's humouring me now, pacifying the monster. "That would appear to be the case. But, as you know, the scene of the accident made it very hard for the the police to confirm..."

Tears surge into my eyes. I don't want to hear that. Harry is dead. My knee is twitching. I try to speak, but there's nothing more to say. He looks into my eyes now.

“It wasn't him you saw just now Rachel. Let's start with that. And it can take time, some considerable time, for these delusions and visions to subside. The mind is a very powerful tool and is perfectly capable of showing you things that don't exist. More often than not it's the very things you fear the most. The medication should help with that, but there is nothing much more we can do to speed up the process. You have suffered a major trauma, witnessed something quite appalling, and the effects can be long-term even with therapy."

I feel flat. I want to please him. I want the treatment to work so I can get ten out of ten, a gold star, move up a level. He reads my mind. Of course he does. He's a psychiatrist.

"Don't be despondent. You are making so much progress," he says.

"Thank you. It doesn't feel like it." Then, as if to prove him wrong, I add "I went to look for Sam yesterday."

"Okay, and…?"

"There was a Sold sign outside her house."

He nods and writes something down before peering at me over his glasses. "And do you remember why?"

I whisper like a child. "She's gone. She died."

"The accident report would indicate that, but as you know the fire was fierce and, well, we have to assume that's the case. And you won't always remember that. You have created a more palatable version of the truth, one that helps you sleep at night. It makes sense, that we protect ourselves from what is too difficult to process. There will be more times that you forget, that you go looking for her, but those times will become less frequent as time goes on. You will, one day, be able to deal with it."

I let the air out of my lungs, breathe through my mouth the way he had taught me, for a count of five, to disspiate the stress. Somewhere down there is the real story of what happened that day in the car park. I try to speak but I can't.

“You can let yourself remember what happened. You're safe here.”

In response, a crack in my mental armour lets the whole scene slide into view. “It was raining. Sam was hiding behind the building. I know he didn’t want us to talk because then he knew I’d find out about what he did to his little boy.” Tears try to come but can’t. The anti-depressants won’t allow it. Instead, new footage plays in my head of Harry pulling Sam towards the car, forcing her into the back seat and slamming the door before screeching away. I could have stopped him. I could have saved her. Pain floods my body. I can't go there. I shut down.

“It wasn't your fault."

But I don’t believe anyone anymore.

Maddie is waiting for me in reception, apologising for not being able to do both journeys this time, asking me how I managed with the cab. I let her lead me by the hand to the lift, and out of the heavy front door into bright daylight. We climb into her little car and soon we are driving past the traffic lights at the World's End. I close my eyes, then force myself to look. The bench is empty. On the pavement, an empty can rolls around in the wind.

Printed in Great Britain
by Amazon